Staring at the Sun

JULIAN BARNES has published eight novels, *Metroland*, *Before She Met Me*, *Flaubert's Parrot*, *Staring at the Sun*, *A History of the World in 10½ Chapters*, *Talking It Over*, *The Porcupine* and *England, England*, a collection of short stories, *Cross Channel*, and one work of non-fiction, *Letters From London 1990–1995*. His work has been translated into more than twenty languages. In France he is the only writer to have won both the Prix Médicis (for *Flaubert's Parrot*) and the Prix Fémina (for *Talking It Over*). In 1993 he was awarded the Shakespeare Prize by the FVS Foundation of Hamburg.

ALSO BY JULIAN BARNES IN PICADOR

Metroland

Before She Met Me

Flaubert's Parrot

A History of the World in 10½ Chapters

Talking It Over

The Porcupine

Letters From London 1990–1995

Cross Channel

JULIAN BARNES

Staring at the Sun

PICADOR

in association with Jonathan Cape

First published 1986 by Jonathan Cape Ltd

This edition published 1987 by Picador
an imprint of Pan Macmillan Ltd
Pan Macmillan, 20 New Wharf Road, London N1 9RR
Basingstoke and Oxford
Associated companies throughout the world
www.panmacmillan.com

In association with Jonathan Cape Ltd

ISBN 0 330 29930 1

23 25 27 29 28 26 24

A CIP catalogue record for this book is available from
the British Library.

Printed and bound in Great Britain by
Mackays of Chatham plc, Chatham, Kent

to Pat

This is what happened. On a calm, black night in June 1941 Sergeant-Pilot Thomas Prosser was poaching over Northern France. His Hurricane IIB was black in its camouflage paint. Inside the cockpit, red light from the instrument panel fell softly on Prosser's hands and face; he glowed like an avenger. He was flying with the hood back, looking towards the ground for the lights of an aerodrome, looking towards the sky for the hot colour of a bomber's exhaust. Prosser was waiting, in the last half-hour before dawn, for a Heinkel or a Dornier on its way back from some English city. The bomber would have skirted anti-aircraft guns, declined the publicity of searchlights, dodged barrage balloons and night fighters; it would be steadying itself, the crew would be thinking of hot coffee fierce with chicory, the landing gear would crunch down — and then would come the poacher's crafty retribution.

There was no prey that night. At 3.46 Prosser set course for base. He crossed the French coast at 18,000 feet. Perhaps disappointment had made him delay his return longer than usual, for as he glanced up the Channel to the east he saw the sun begin to rise. The air was empty and serene as the orange sun extracted itself calmly and steadily from the sticky yellow bar of the horizon. Prosser followed its slow exposure. Out of trained instinct, his head jerked on his neck every three seconds, but it seems unlikely he would have spotted a German fighter had there been one. All he could take in was the sun rising from the sea: stately, inexorable, almost comic.

Finally, when the orange globe sat primly on th

distant waves, Prosser looked away. He became aware of danger again; his black aeroplane in the bright morning air was now as conspicuous as some Arctic predator caught in the wrong fur by a change of season. As he banked and turned, banked and turned, he glimpsed below him a long trail of black smoke. A solitary ship, perhaps in trouble. He descended quickly towards the twinkling, miniature waves, until at last he could make out a tubby merchantman heading west. But the black smoke had stopped, and there seemed nothing wrong; probably she had just been stoking up.

At 8,000 feet Prosser flattened out and set fresh course for base. Half-way across the Channel he allowed himself, like the German bomber crews, to think about hot coffee, and the bacon sandwich he would eat after debriefing. Then something happened. The speed of his descent had driven the sun back below the horizon, and as he looked towards the east he saw it rise again: the same sun coming up from the same place across the same sea. Once more, Prosser put aside caution and just watched: the orange globe, the yellow bar, the horizon's shelf, the serene air, and the smooth, weightless lift of the sun as it rose from the waves for the second time that morning. It was an ordinary miracle he would never forget.

ONE

You ask me what life is? It is like asking what a carrot is. A carrot is a carrot, and nothing more is known.
Chekhov to Olga Knipper, 20 April 1904

progress. She thought about them frequently, and wondered what a hyacinth looked like. Time for Slide 2. In late January she went to the bathroom with a torch, turned off the light, took down the pot, unscrewed a tiny viewing-hole, aimed the torch and quickly looked inside. The four promising tips were still there, still half an inch long. At least the light she had let in at Christmas hadn't harmed them.

In late February she looked again; but obviously the growing season hadn't started yet. Three weeks later Uncle Leslie called by on his way to play golf. Over lunch he turned to her conspiratorially and asked, 'Well, little Jeanie, are the hyacinths hyacinth Christmas?'

'You told me not to look.'

'So I did. So I did.'

She looked again at the end of March, then — Slides 5 to 10 — on April the second, fifth, eighth, ninth, tenth and eleventh. On the twelfth her mother agreed to a closer examination of the pot. They laid yesterday's *Daily Express* on the kitchen table, and carefully unwrapped the brown paper. The four ochre sprouts had not advanced at all. Mrs Serjeant looked uneasy.

'I think we'd better throw them out, Jean.' Adults were always throwing things out. That was clearly one of the big differences. Children liked keeping things.

'Maybe the roots are growing.' Jean started easing away at the peaty earth packed tight against the tips.

'I shouldn't do that,' said Mother. But it was too late. One after the other, Jean dug out four upturned wooden golf tees.

Strangely, the Incident didn't make her lose faith in Uncle Leslie. Instead, she lost faith in hyacinths.

Looking back, Jean assumed that she must have had friends as a chi' but she couldn't recall that special confidante with the w or the playground games with skipping-rope and ecret messages passed along ink-stained desks at a h a daunting stone inscription above its door. all these things; perhaps not. In retrospect, riend enough. He had crinkly hair which

6

he kept well Brylcreemed, and a dark blue blazer with a regimental badge on the breast pocket. He knew how to make wine glasses out of sweet papers, and whenever he went to the golf club he always called it 'popping down the Old Green Heaven'. Uncle Leslie was the sort of man she would marry.

Shortly after the hyacinth Incident, he began taking her down the Old Green Heaven. When they arrived he would sit her on a mildewed bench near the car-park and instruct her with mock severity to guard his clubs.

'Just going to wash behind the old ear-pieces.'

Twenty minutes later they would set off towards the first tee, Uncle Leslie carrying his clubs and smelling of beer, Jean with the sand-iron over her shoulder. This was a good-luck ploy devised by Leslie: as long as Jeanie was carrying the sand-iron in readiness, the lightning would be diverted and he would be kept out of the bunker.

'Don't let the club-head drop,' he would say, 'or there'll be more sand flying than on a windy day in the Gobi desert.' And she would shoulder the club correctly, like a rifle. Once, feeling tired at the uphill fifteenth, she had trailed it behind her off the tee, and Uncle Leslie's second shot squirted straight into a bunker fifteen yards away.

'Now look what you've done,' he said; though he seemed almost as pleased as he was cross. 'Have to buy me one at the nineteenth for that.'

Uncle Leslie often talked to her in a funny code she pretended to understand. Everyone knew there were only eighteen holes on a golf course, and that she didn't have any money, but she nodded as if she was always buying people one — one what? — at the nineteenth. When she grew up, someone would explain the code to her; though in the meantime she felt quite happy not knowing. And there were bits she understood already. If the ball swerved disobediently off into the woods, Leslie would sometimes mutter, 'One for the hyacinths' — the only reference he ever made to his Christmas present.

But mostly his remarks were beyond her. They marched

purposefully down the fairway, he with his bagful of quietly clanking hickory, she sloping arms with the sand-iron. Jean was not allowed to speak: Uncle Leslie had explained that chatter put him off thinking about his next shot. He, on the other hand, was permitted to talk; and as they strode towards that distant white glint which sometimes turned out to be a sweet paper, he would occasionally stop, bend down and whisper to her the secrets of his mind. At the fifth he told her that tomatoes were the cause of cancer, and that the sun would never set on the Empire; at the tenth she learned that bombers were the future, and that old Musso might be an Eytie but he knew which way the paper folded. Once they had stopped on the short twelfth (an unprecedented act on a par three) while Leslie gravely explained, 'Besides, your *Jew* doesn't really *enjoy* golf.'

Then they had continued towards the bunker on the left of the green, with Jean repeating to herself this suddenly awarded truth.

She liked going down the Old Green Heaven; you never knew quite what would happen. Once, after Uncle Leslie had washed behind his ears more thoroughly than usual, he had crackled off into the deep rough alongside the fourth. She was made to turn her back, but couldn't avoid hearing a prolonged splashing noise of remarkable volume and implications. She had peered under a raised elbow (it didn't count as looking), and seen steam rising amid the waist-high bracken.

Next there was Leslie's trick. Between the ninth green and the tenth tee, surrounded by newly planted silver birches, was a little wooden hut like a rustic bird-box. Here, if the wind was in the right direction, Uncle Leslie would sometimes do his trick. From the breast pocket of his tweed jacket with the leather elbows he would take a cigarette, lay it on his knee, pass his hands over it like a magician, put it in his mouth, give Jeanie a slow wink, and strike a match. She would sit beside him trying to hold her breath, trying not to be a shufflebottom. Huffers and puffers spoiled tricks, Uncle Leslie had said, and so did shufflebottoms.

8

After a minute or two she would ease her glance sideways, taking care not to move suddenly. The cigarette had an inch of ash on it, and Uncle Leslie was taking another puff. At the next glance, his head was tipped slightly back, and half the cigarette consisted of ash. From this point on, Uncle Leslie wouldn't look at her; instead, he would concentrate very carefully, slowly leaning back a little more with each puff he took. Finally, his head would be at right-angles to his spine, with the cigarette, now pure ash apart from the last half-inch where Leslie was holding it, rising vertically towards the roof of the giant bird-box. The trick had worked.

Then he would reach out his left hand and touch her upper arm; she would get up quietly, trying not to breathe in case she huffed and puffed the ash down Leslie's jacket with the leather elbows, and go ahead to the tenth tee. A couple of minutes later Leslie would rejoin her, smiling a little. She never asked how he did his trick; perhaps she thought he wouldn't tell her.

And then there was the screaming. This always happened in the same place, a field behind the triangle of damp, smelly beeches which pushed their way in to the dogleg fourteenth. On each occasion, Uncle Leslie had sliced his drive so badly that they had to search the least visited part of the wood, where the trunks had moss on them and the beech-nuts were thicker on the ground. The first time, they had found themselves by a stile, which was slimy to the touch though the weather had been dry for days. They climbed the stile and began hunting in the first few yards of sloping meadowland. After some rather aimless kicking and club-scuffling, Leslie had bent down and said, 'Why don't we have a good old scream?'

She smiled back at him. Having a good old scream was clearly something people did on these occasions. After all, it was very annoying not to be able to find the ball. Leslie explained further. 'When you're all screamed out you have to fall down. That's the rules.'

Then they had put their heads back and screamed at the sky. Uncle Leslie deep and throaty, like a train coming out of a

9

tunnel; Jean high and wavering, uncertain how long her breath would last. You kept your eyes open — that seemed to be an unstated rule — and stared hard up at the sky, daring it to answer your challenge. Then you took your second breath, and screamed again, more confidently, more insistently. Then again, and in the pause for each fresh breath Leslie's train noises swelled and roared; and then exhaustion arrived suddenly, and you had no scream left, and you fell to the ground. She would have fallen anyway, even if it hadn't been in the rules; fatigue raced through her body like a tidal bore.

There was a thump as Uncle Leslie flopped down a few yards away, and they stared their parallel, heaving stares up at the quiet sky. Half-way to heaven, a few small clouds shifted gently, as if reluctantly tethered; but perhaps even this movement was given them only by the panting of the two supine figures. It was clearly in the rules that you could pant as hard as you liked.

After a while, she heard Leslie cough.

'Well,' he said, 'I think I'll allow myself a free drop.' And they trailed back across the slimy stile, through the crackly beech-nuts to the angle of the fourteenth where Uncle Leslie, after looking around for spies, calmly thumbed a tee into the fairway, popped a gleaming new ball on top, and struck a brassie some two hundred yards to the green. This despite being all screamed out, thought Jean.

They went screaming only when Leslie sliced his ball very badly off the tee, which seemed to happen when the course was empty. And they didn't do it too often, because after the first occasion Jean got the whooping cough. Getting the whooping cough hadn't qualified as an Incident, but Uncle Leslie's whip-round had. Or rather, the result of Uncle Leslie's whip-round.

She was in bed on the fourth day of her illness, occasionally giving the throaty cry of some exotic bird lost in a foreign sky, when he dropped in. He sat on her bed in his blazer with the badge, smelling a bit as if he'd been washing behind his ears, and instead of asking how she felt, murmured, 'You didn't tell them about the screaming?'

Of course she hadn't.

'Only you see, it's a secret, after all. Rather a good secret, it seems to me.'

Jean nodded. It was a remarkably good secret. But perhaps the screaming had caused the whooping cough. Her mother was always telling her to guard against over-excitement. Maybe she had over-excited her throat by screaming, and it had started whooping as a result. Uncle Leslie behaved as if he suspected things might be his fault. As she gave her panicking bird-call, he looked a little shifty.

Two days later Mrs Serjeant put Jean's winter underwear on the edge of the bed, then a thick dress, her winter coat, a scarf and a blanket. She seemed displeased but resigned.

'Come on. Uncle Leslie's had a whip-round.' Uncle Leslie's whip-round, Jean discovered, included a taxi. Her first taxi. On the way to the aerodrome she took care not to appear over-excited. At Hendon her mother stayed in the car. Jean took her father's hand, while he explained to her that the wooden parts of a De Havilland were made of spruce. Spruce was a very hard wood, he said, almost as hard as the metal parts of the aeroplane, so she was not to worry. She had not been worrying.

Sixty-minute sightseeing tour of London; departures on the hour. Among the dozen passengers were two more children wrapped up like parcels although it was only August; perhaps their uncles had had whip-rounds as well. Her father sat across the aisle and stopped her when she tried to lean past him and look out: the point of the flight, he explained, was medical, not educational. He spent the whole trip gazing at the back of the wicker seat in front of him and holding on to his knee-caps. He seemed as if he might get over-excited at any minute. When the De Havilland banked, Jean could see, beyond its chubby engines and the criss-cross of the struts, something that might be Tower Bridge. She turned to her father.

'Shh,' he said, 'I'm concentrating on getting you better.'

It was almost a year before she and Uncle Leslie went screaming again. They popped down the Old Green Heaven, of course; but somehow Leslie's driving at the dogleg fourteenth had acquired a new accuracy. When, finally, the next summer, he drew the club-head across the face of the ball and produced a high, wailing slice, the ball seemed to know exactly where it was meant to go. So did they: through the long rough, across the damp beech wood, over the slimy stile, and into the sloping meadowland. They screamed into the warm air, and thumped down on their backs. Jean found herself scanning the sky for aeroplanes. She rolled her eyes round in their sockets, and searched to the edge of her vision. No clouds, and no aeroplanes: it was as if she and Uncle Leslie had emptied the sky with their noise. Nothing but blue.

'Well,' said Leslie, 'I think I'll award myself a free drop.' They had not looked for his ball on their way through the wood, and they did not look for it on the way back either.

The third time they went screaming, there was an aeroplane. Jean hadn't noticed it while they were bawling at the heavens; but when they were supine and panting, and the clouds were bobbing on their tethers, she became aware of a distant buzzing. Too regular to be an insect; sounding both near and distant at the same time. It appeared, briefly and more noisily, between two clouds, then vanished, reappeared, and buzzed slowly towards the horizon, losing height. She imagined chubby engines, whistling struts, and children wrapped like parcels.

'When Lindbergh flew the Atlantic,' Leslie commented from a few feet away, 'he had five sandwiches with him. He only ate one and a half.'

'What happened to the others?'

'What others?'

'The other three and a half.'

Uncle Leslie stood up; he looked moody. Perhaps she wasn't allowed to talk, even though they weren't on the fairway. Finally, as they scuffled in the beech-nuts, this time looking for the ball, he said, in an irritated mutter, 'They're probably in a sandwich museum.'

A sandwich museum, Jean wondered to herself: were there

such things? But she knew not to ask any further. And gradually, over the next couple of holes, Leslie's mood improved. On the seventeenth, after a quick look up and down the fairway, he became conspiratorial again.

'Shall we play the Shoelace Game?'

He'd never mentioned it before, but she agreed at once.

Blatantly, Uncle Leslie kicked his ball across to the short rough. When they caught up with it, he bent down and took off his brown-and-white co-respondent shoes. He laid the loose ends of the laces in a cross on the middle of the inner sole, looked at her and nodded. She took off her black walking shoes and did the same. She watched as, with a comic formality, he worked first his toes, then the rest of his feet, back into his shoes. She did the same; he winked, bent down on one knee like a suitor, patted her calf, and slowly tugged both laces out from the soft underside of her left foot. Jean giggled. It felt wonderful. Ticklish at first, and gradually more ticklish but with a thrust of pleasure pushing right up into her stomach. She closed her eyes, and Uncle Leslie, with a teasing pull, eased the laces out from underneath her right foot. It was even better with your eyes closed.

Then it was his turn. She crouched down at his feet. His shoes seemed enormous from this distance. His socks smelt distantly of the barnyard.

'One at a time for me,' he whispered, and she seized the first lace close to where it disappeared into its eyelet. She pulled; nothing happened; she pulled again, more sharply; he wiggled his foot, and the lace came suddenly free.

'No good,' he said. 'Too quick. Put it back.'

He arched his foot, and she poked the long brown lace back into his shoe, between his damp sock and the inner sole. Then she pulled again, more smoothly; the lace came out with slow ease, and from the silence overhead she deduced that she had done it correctly. One by one, she pulled the other three ends of his laces. He patted her on the head.

'I think a little seven iron, don't you? Toss it up, bit of backspin, Bob's your uncle.'

'Can we do it again?'

'Certainly not.' He addressed the ball, shuffled his feet as if he'd still got the laces trapped, and waggled the club-head with loose wrists. 'Got to let the batteries recharge, haven't we?' She nodded; he pushed the ball a few inches on to a mossier clump of grass where it sat up well, fiddled his feet some more, struck a clean shot towards the flag and set off down the fairway. 'Laces!' he shouted back at her, and she stooped to tie them up.

But they did play the Shoelace Game again, quite often. Not always at the Old Green Heaven; sometimes, rather suddenly and furtively, when they were at home. The rules were always the same: Uncle Leslie went first, and pulled out both laces; she went second, and tugged one at a time. Once she tried to play it by herself; but it was not the same. She wondered if the game made you ill. Everything nice was supposed to make you ill. Chocolates, cakes, figs made you ill; screaming gave you the whooping cough. What did the Shoelace Game give you?

Presumably she would find out the answer to that quite soon. And then, as she grew up, she would find out the other answers. Answers to all sorts of questions. How to decide which club to use. Whether there was a sandwich museum. Why your Jews didn't enjoy golf. Whether her father had been frightened in the De Havilland, or just concentrating. How that Musso knew which way the paper folded. Why food looked quite different when it came out at the other end of your body. How to smoke a cigarette without the ash falling off it. Whether Heaven was up the chimney, as she secretly suspected. And why the mink was excessively tenacious of life.

Jean didn't even understand what was meant by that last phrase; but in time she might discover the question, and later she might discover the answer. She knew about the mink because of Aunt Evelyn's prints. There were two of them, left behind years earlier with a promise of early collection, and subsequently shuffled from wall to wall. In the end, they were put in Jean's room. Father wondered if one of them wasn't unsuitable; but

Mother insisted that Evelyn's pictures stay together. It was only honest, she said.

The horizontal picture showed two men in a forest somewhere; they wore old-fashioned clothes and hats. The one with the beard was holding up a ferret by the scruff of its neck, while the other man, the one without the beard, leaned on his gun. There was a pile of dead ferrets at his feet. Except that they weren't ferrets, because the title of the picture was Mink Trapping; and underneath was a story Jean had read many times.

The Mink, like the musk-rat and ermine long-tailed weasel, does not possess much cunning, and is easily captured in any kind of trap; it is taken in steel-traps and box-traps, but more generally in what are called dead-falls. It is attracted by any kind of flesh, but we have usually seen the traps baited with the head of a ruffed-grouse, wild duck, chicken, jay, or other bird. The Mink is excessively tenacious of life, and we had found it still alive under a dead-fall, with a pole lying across its body pressed down by a weight of 150 lbs, beneath which it had been struggling for nearly twenty-four hours.

'Excessively tenacious of life' was not the only part she didn't yet understand. What was a ruffed-grouse? Or a musk-rat? She knew what a wild duck was, and there had been a pair of barking jays last Spring in the beech wood at the dogleg fourteenth, and they had chicken for Sunday lunch when her father had done a customer a favour. Mrs Baxter would come in to pluck and draw it for her mother in the morning, and would call back at about five o'clock for one of the legs, which would be wrapped in greaseproof paper. Jean's father liked to make jokes about Mrs Baxter's leg while he was carving; jokes which made his daughter giggle and his wife purse her lips.

'Does Mrs Baxter have the head as well?' Jean once asked.

'No dear. Why?'

'What do you do with it?'

'Throw it in the dustbin.'

'Shouldn't you keep it to sell to the mink trappers?'

'You just get them to call, my girl,' replied her father jovially. 'You just get them to call.'

The vertical print in Jean's room showed a ladder set up against a tree, with words painted on the rungs. INDUSTRY said the bottom rung; TEMPERANCE said the second, though really it only said TEMPERAN, because the last two letters were cut off by the knee of the ladder-climber. Then came PRUDENCE, INTEGRITY, ECONOMY, PUNCTUALITY, COURAGE and, the top rung, PERSEVER-ANCE. In the foreground people were queueing to climb the tree, which had Christmas balls hanging from its leaves, with more words written on them like 'Happiness', 'Honor', 'the Favor of God' and 'Good will to Men'. In the background were people who didn't want to climb the tree; they were gambling, swindling, betting, going on strike and entering a large building called Stock Exchange.

Jean understood the general intention of the picture, though sometimes she absently confused this tree with the Tree of Knowledge, which she had heard about in Scripture. The Tree of Knowledge was clearly a bad thing to have climbed; this tree was clearly a good thing, even if she didn't really understand all the words on the rungs, or the two written on the main shafts of the ladder: MORALITY, said one, HONESTY, the other. Some of the words she thought she understood. Honesty meant keeping Aunt Evelyn's two pictures together, and not moving your ball to a better position when no one was looking; Punctuality meant not being late for school; Economy was what her father did at the shop and her mother did at home; Courage — well, Courage was going up in aeroplanes. She would doubtless understand the other words in time.

* * * *

Jean was seventeen when the war began, and the event made her feel relieved. Things had all been taken out of her hands; she no longer needed to feel guilty. For the preceding few years her father had taken the full weight of various political crises firmly on his shoulders; that was his duty, after all, as Head of the Household. He would read the news to them from the *Daily Express*, with pauses after each paragraph, and explain the bulletins on the wireless. It often felt to Jean as if her father owned a small family business which was being threatened by a gang of foreigners with outlandish names, illegal business methods and cut-throat pricing. Her mother knew all the right responses; she knew the different noises to make when names like Beneš, Daladier and Litvinov came up, and when it was best to throw up her hands in confusion and let Father explain it to her again from the beginning. Jean tried to be interested, but it sounded to her like a story which had begun a long time ago, even before she was born, and which she would never completely master. At first she used to keep silent at the names of those sinister foreign businessmen with their lorry-loads of stolen digestive biscuits and poached pheasants; but even silence wasn't safe — it suggested lack of proper concern — so she would occasionally ask questions. The trouble was, how could you know what questions to ask? It seemed to her that you were in a position to ask a really correct question only if you already knew the answer, and what was the point in that? Once, coming out of a bored reverie, she had asked Father about this new woman prime minister of Austria called Ann Schluss. That had been a mistake.

War, of course, was men's business. Men conducted it, and men — tapping out their pipes like headmasters — explained it. What had women done in the Great War? Given out white feathers, stoned dachshunds, gone out to nurse in France. First they sent men off to fight, then they patched them up. Was it likely to be any different this time? Probably not.

Even so, Jean felt obscurely that her inability to understand the European crisis was partly responsible for its continuation. She felt guilty about Munich. She felt guilty about the Sudetenland. She felt guilty about the Nazi-Soviet Non-Aggression Pact. If only she could remember whether you could trust the French or not. Was Poland more important than Czechoslovakia? And what was this about Palestine? Palestine was in the desert and the Jews wanted to go there. Well, at least this confirmed what Uncle Leslie said about Jews: that they didn't like golf anyway. Nobody who liked golf would choose to go and live in the desert. It would be like playing out of the bunker all the time. Perhaps the golf courses out there had fairways made of sand and bunkers made of grass.

So when the war began, Jean was relieved. It was all Hitler's fault: it was nothing to do with her. And at least it meant that something was happening. The war counted as another Incident: this was how she viewed it at first. The men were called up, Mother joined the WVS, and Jean was finally allowed to cut off the broad yellow-brown plait which had run down her back for so many years. Her father mourned its loss, but was persuaded that the saving on soap and water when Jean washed her hair would significantly help the war effort. Sentimentally, he asked for the plait when it was cut, and kept it on a shelf in his potting shed for several weeks, until his wife threw it out.

There had been secret discussions among the Serjeants about whether Jean should get a job; but with Mother joining the WVS it was thought she would be better off keeping house. 'Good practice, girl,' said her father with a wink. Good practice: not that she felt in any way up to whatever it was she was practising for. When she looked at her parents, she was daunted by how grown-up they were. How long would it take before she was as grown-up as that?

They knew their own minds; they had opinions; they could tell right from wrong. She felt she could tell right from wrong only because she had been repeatedly informed of the difference; her opinions were twitching, vulnerable tadpoles compared with the honking frogs that were her parents' views; while as for knowing your own mind, this seemed a bewildering process. How could you know your own mind without using your mind to discover your mind in the first place? A dog circling in pursuit of its own cropped tail. Jean felt tired at the very thought.

The other part of growing up was getting to look like

someone. Her father, who managed the grocery at Bryden, looked like a man who managed a grocery: he was round and neat, hitched up his sleeves with a pair of elasticated steel bands, and seemed as if he was kind but had a reserve of severity — the sort of man who knew that a pound of flour was a pound of flour and not fifteen ounces, who could tell which biscuits were in which square tin without even looking at the label, and who could put his hand close, oh so close, to the whirring bacon-slicer without shaving the skin from his palm.

Jean's mother also looked like someone, with her pointy nose and rather protuberant blue eyes, with her hair caught back in a bun during the daytime when she wore her bottle-green-and-claret WVS uniform, or loose in the evenings when she listened to Father and knew exactly what questions to ask. She had gone on salvage drives and helped collect thousands of tin cans; she had spent weeks threading strips of coloured fabric through camouflage netting ('Just like making a huge carpet, Jean'); she had baled paper, filled in at the mobile canteen, packed vegetable hampers for minesweepers. No wonder she knew her own mind; no wonder she looked like someone.

Jean would sometimes stare into the mirror, inspecting herself for signs of change; but her straight hair lay sullenly flat on her head, and her blue eyes were marred by silly flecks. An article in the *Daily Express* had explained that many film stars in Hollywood were successful because their faces were heart-shaped. Well, there was no hope for that now; she was far too square-jawed. If only these bits of her face would start looking as if they belonged together. Oh *do* get on with it, she sometimes whispered at the mirror. Mother once caught her at self-examination and commented, 'You're not pretty, but you'll do.'

I'll do, she thought. My parents think I'll do. But would anybody else? She missed Uncle Leslie. They weren't allowed to talk about him nowadays, but she often thought of him; he had always been on her side. Once, they'd been walking up the long tenth at the Old Green Heaven, Jean carrying the sand-iron in the good-luck position, and she'd asked him, 'What will I do when I grow up?'

It had seemed natural to ask, natural to assume that he would be more likely to know than she. Uncle Leslie, with his brown-and-white co-respondent shoes and his quietly rattling clubs, had taken the head of the sand-iron and waggled it from side to side on her shoulder. Then he put his hand on the back of her neck and murmured, 'The sky's the limit, little Jeanie. The sky's the limit.'

Not much happened in the war at first, it seemed to Jean; but then it got going, and people started to be killed. She also began to understand it better: who was trying to run Father out of business, and the names of his shifty associates. She felt fiercely about these foreigners with their underhand tricks. She saw a fat thumb with a dirty nail pressing down on the scales. Perhaps she ought to join up. But Father thought she was doing more good where she was. 'Keep the home fires burning,' he said.

And then the war brought Tommy Prosser. That was definitely an Incident. The billeting papers arrived on a Tuesday, the Wednesday was spent complaining that there wasn't enough room for the three of them, let alone four, and on the Thursday Tommy Prosser arrived. He was a short, slim man in RAF uniform, with black hair brilliantined down and a little black moustache. The case under his arm was circled by a leather strap. He looked sideways at Jean as she opened the door, then glanced away, smiled at the wall, and announced, as if to a superior officer, 'Sergeant-Pilot Prosser.'

'Oh. Yes. They said.'

'Very good of you and all that.'

His tone was expressionless, but his unfamiliar Northern accent sounded scratchy to Jean, like a rough shirt.

'Oh. Yes. Mother will be home at five.'

'Would you like me to come back then?'

'I don't know.' Why didn't she know anything? He was going to live with them, so presumably it made sense to ask him in. But then what happened? Would he expect tea or something?

'It's all right. I'll come back at five.' He looked at her, glanced away, smiled at the wall, and walked off down the path. From the kitchen window Jean saw him sitting on the verge across the road, staring at his case. At four o'clock it began to rain, and she asked him in.

He'd been posted up from West Malling. No, he didn't know how long for. No, he couldn't tell her why. No, not Spitfires, Hurricanes. Oh dear, already she was asking the wrong questions. She pointed up the stairs to where his room was, uncertain whether it was rude not to accompany him, or forward to do so. Prosser didn't seem to mind. Apart from his name, he had volunteered no information, asked no questions, commented on nothing, not even the way everything was freshly polished and smelt nice. They had given him the box room. There hadn't been time to decorate it, of course, but they had hung Aunt Evelyn's pictures on the wall for him.

He kept to his room most of the time, appearing punctually for meals and answering Father's questions. It was odd to have two men in the house. At first Father deferred to Sergeant-Pilot Prosser; he enquired with tactful admiration about the life of an airman, spoke with comradely contempt of 'Jerry', and would jokingly instruct Mother to 'Give another helping to our hero of the stratosphere'. But Prosser didn't seem to answer Father's questions in the right spirit; he accepted extra helpings without the extravagant thanks Mother clearly expected; and though he willingly helped with the blackout curtains, he appeared slothful in discussions about North African strategy. It became clear to Jean that Prosser was a disappointment to Father; equally clear that he knew it, and didn't mind. Perhaps they just weren't asking him the right questions yet. Perhaps heroes who flew Hurricanes required special questions. Or maybe it was that he came from another part of the country: somewhere in Lancashire, near Blackburn, he said. Perhaps they had different ways of behaving up there.

Occasionally, when they were alone in the house, Prosser would come down, lean against the kitchen door, and watch her ironing, or making bread, or polishing the knives. At first she felt embarrassed, but then less so; having a witness to her tasks made her feel more useful. Talking to him wasn't any easier when her parents were out, though. He didn't always answer questions; he could get prickly; sometimes he would simply look away and smile, as if remembering some aerial manoeuvre she couldn't possibly understand.

One day, as she was cleaning the stove, he announced crossly, 'I'm grounded, you see.'

She looked up, but before she could reply, he went on, 'I used to be called Sun-Up. Sun-Up Prosser.'

'I see.' This seemed a safe answer. She went back to smearing brown oven-paste on the inside of the stove. Prosser stamped off to his room.

For several weeks, the atmosphere in the house was uneasy. This is just like the Phoney War, Jean thought; except that there probably wouldn't be any fighting at the end of it. There wasn't. Father increasingly confided his views on military affairs only to Mother, while he would occasionally hint to Jean that just because someone was living under your roof it didn't mean you had to be friendly. Civil was all that was required.

* * * *

Tommy Prosser came downstairs one afternoon at four. Jean was making a pot of tea.

'Something to eat?' she said, still uncertain about the billeting regulations.

'How about an All Clear sandwich?'

'What's that?'

'Never heard of an All Clear sandwich? And you surrounded by all the necessaries?' She shook her head. 'You stir the pot and I'll rustle one up.'

After a little banging of doors and some whistling with his back turned to her, Prosser produced two sandwiches on a plate. The bread did not look as if it had been cut with an entirely steady hand. Jean had tasted many better sandwiches, she had to admit; she tried to sound fair but encouraging.

'Why's mine got dandelion leaves in?'

'Because it's an All Clear sandwich.' Prosser grinned at her and looked sharply away. 'Fish paste, marge and dandelion leaves. Of course, the quality of the local dandelions may not be up to scratch. You can send it back to the kitchen if you don't like it.'

'It's . . . lovely. I'm sure it'll grow on me.'

'I'm sure I'll fly again,' he replied, as if giving the second half of a joke.

'Oh, I'm *sure* you will.'

'*I'm* sure *I* will,' he repeated with sudden sarcasm, as if what he really wanted to do was slap her. Oh dear. Jean felt stupid and ashamed. She looked down at her plate. There was a silence.

'Did you know', she said, 'that when Lindbergh flew the Atlantic he took five sandwiches with him?'

Prosser grunted.

'And that he only ate one and a half?'

Prosser grunted again. With no obvious interest in his voice, he asked, 'What happened to the rest?'

'That's what I always wanted to know. Perhaps they're in a sandwich museum somewhere.'

There was a silence. Jean felt she had wasted the story. It was one of her best, and she had wasted it. She wouldn't ever be able to tell him that story again. She should have kept it for when he was in a better mood. It was all her fault. The silence continued.

'I suppose you know where Lindbergh's plane is,' she finally said in the bright tone of one who has taken conversation lessons. 'I mean, *that* must be in a museum.'

'It's not a plane,' said Prosser. 'It's never a plane. It's an *aero*-plane. *Aero*plane. All right?'

'Yes,' she replied. He might as well have slapped her. Aeroplane, aeroplane, aeroplane.

Eventually, Prosser gave a short cough, the noise of one moving from anger or embarrassment to some other focus of emotion.

'I'll tell you the most beautiful thing I've ever seen,' he said in a tense, almost grumpy voice. Jean, half-expecting some arch compliment, kept her head ducked down. She still hadn't eaten her other piece of sandwich.

'I was on night ops. In the summer — June. Flying with the hood back, everything black and quiet. Well, quiet as you get.' Jean lifted her head. 'It's . . . ' He stopped. 'You wouldn't know about night vision, would you?' This time, his tone was kindly. It was all right if she didn't know; it wasn't like calling an aeroplane a plane.

'You eat all those carrots,' she said, and heard him chuckle.

'Yes, we do. That's what we get called sometimes, the carrot-eaters. But it's not to do with that really. It's technical. It's the colour of your instrument lights. They have to be red, you see. Normally they're green and white, but green and white kills your night vision. Can't see a thing. They have to be red — red's the only colour that works.

'So you see, it's all black and red up there. The night's black, the aeroplane's black, it's all red in the cockpit — it even turns your hands and face red — and you're looking out for red exhausts. You're alone as well. That was a good part. Off by yourself, solo, over to France. Just when their bombers were getting back from their missions, from bombing us. You'd hang around one of their dromes, or you might shuttle between a pair of them if they were close enough. You'd be waiting for the landing lights to come on — or maybe you'd pick up something from its navigation lights. A Heinkel or a Dornier, that was the usual. You might get the odd Focke-Wulf.

'What you could do was this.' Prosser chuckled briefly. 'When they came in they'd always do a circuit first. Like this; descend, approach, fly down the runway, do a left-hand circuit, always a left-hand, come in again and land.' With his right arm Prosser sketched the German bomber's flight-path. 'What you could do, if you were feeling a bit cheeky, was come in at about the same time, and when he flew his left-hand circuit, you'd fly a right-hand one.' With his other arm Prosser traced the Hurricane's path. 'Then, smack as he came out of his circuit, flaps down, just above stalling speed, and he was thinking about that last bit of turn and then getting the crate safely down, you'd be coming out of your circuit.' Prosser's curving hands stopped opposite one another, the fingertips gunning from close range. 'Bam. Sitting duck. Barn door. And the buggers thought they were safely home. Poaching, that's what we called it. Poaching.'

Jean felt distantly flattered that he was telling her about his flying days, but kept it to herself. She did the same with her feelings about the unfairness of poaching. Even if the Heinkel was full of black marketeers back from bombing London or Coventry or wherever. She hadn't approved of poaching since she'd first lived with Aunt Evelyn's print of the mink trappers. It had been right to put it in Prosser's room. And was the Heinkel tenacious of life?

'If you downed one, you beat it. There'd be quite a bit of dirt if you hung around. You only had about twenty minutes over there, in any case.' Prosser's story seemed to be ending; then he suddenly remembered what it was he'd meant to say. 'Anyway. One night, I hadn't had a sniff of anything. Drawn a blank. Nothing doing. Crossed the Channel higher than usual, about 18,000. I must have left it later than I should because it was starting to get light. Maybe the nights were still getting shorter.

'Anyway. There I was, looking up the Channel, and the sun was just starting to come up. It was one of those mornings . . . well, it's hard to describe unless you've been up there yourself.'

'I went up in a De Havilland for the whooping cough,' said Jean, rather proudly. 'But it was a long time ago. When I was eight or nine.'

Prosser took the interruption without offence. 'It's so clear, it's clearer than words can say. No clouds, the sniff of morning air, and this huge orange sun coming up. I just watched it, and then, after a couple of minutes, it was all there — this bloody big orange sitting on top of the drink looking all pleased with itself.

'I was so happy I could have had a 109 up my tail and I wouldn't have noticed. I'd just been tooling along, staring at the sun. So I had a good squint round. Nothing there, just me and the sun. Not a whiff of cloud, and you could see straight down to the Channel. There was a ship there, tiny speck, lots of black smoke coming out of it; so I checked the fuel and went down to take a dekko. It was a merchantman.' Prosser narrowed his eyes in memory. 'About a 10,000-tonner, I'd guess. Anyway, there was nothing wrong. She was probably just stoking up. So I headed back to base. I must have lost half my height, down to eight or nine. And then, guess what? I'd descended so quickly, you see, that it all happened all over again: this bloody great orange sun started popping up from under the horizon. Couldn't believe my eyes. All over again. Like running a film back and having another look at it. I'd have done it a third time and come home at nought feet except I'd have ended up in the drink. Didn't want to join the submarine boys that fast.'

'It sounds wonderful.' Jean wasn't sure if she was allowed to ask questions. It was a bit like being down at the Old Green Heaven with Uncle Leslie. 'What . . . what else do you miss?'

'Oh, I don't miss *that*,' he replied, quite rudely. 'I don't *miss* that. There's no future in seeing *that* again. It's a miracle, isn't it. You don't want to go back and see miracles again, do you. I'm just glad I saw it when I did. "I've seen the sun rise twice," I'd say to them. "Oh, yes, have the other half." They used to call me Sun-Up Prosser. Some of them did. Until we got posted.'

He stood up and scoffed the piece of sandwich on her plate without asking. 'What I *miss*,' he said emphatically, 'since you want to know, is killing Germans. I used to enjoy that. Chasing them down until they were too low to bale out and then letting them have it. That gave me a lot of satisfaction.' Prosser seemed determined to sound brutal. 'I got in an argument once with a 109 over the Channel. He could turn a bit tighter, but we were pretty well matched. We scrapped around but neither of us could really get in close enough to press the tit. So after a while he broke off, waggled his wings and headed back to base. If he hadn't waggled his wings I wouldn't have minded so much.

26

Who d'you think you are? Bloody knight in armour? All good friends and jolly good company?

'I grabbed a bit of height. There wasn't any sun I could use, but I think he didn't expect me to be chasing him. Expected me to go home like a good chap, have a slap-up meal and play a round of golf, I expect. I gradually began to gain on him — maybe he was nursing his fuel or something. Mind you, I was bumping along like a goods train by the time I lined him up. Gave him about eight seconds, I should think. Saw bits fly off his wing. Didn't knock him down, more's the pity, but I think he knew what I thought of him.'

Sun-Up Prosser turned and stomped out of the room. Jean fished a piece of dandelion from between her teeth and chewed it. She had been right. It did taste sour.

After this, Prosser took to coming down and talking to her. Usually, she carried on with her tasks while he stood propped against the door. This seemed to make it easier for both of them.

'I was at Eastleigh,' he began once, as she crouched by the grate rolling the *Express* into firelighters. 'Watching this little Skua take off. Bit gusty, not enough to stop flying or anything. The Skua, as I shouldn't think you're aware, takes off with a funny sort of tail-down technique, and I thought I'd watch it go, cheer myself up or something. Well, it scuttled along the runway, and was getting up to flying speed, when it hopped into the air, suddenly, then flipped over on its back. It didn't look too bad — just upside down. A few of us ran across the tarmac thinking we might be able to pull the chaps out. When we got half-way there we saw something on the runway. It was the pilot's head.' Prosser looked across at Jean but she kept her back to him and went on folding newspaper. 'Then we got a bit nearer and there was another. It must have happened as the Skua flipped over. You wouldn't believe how neat it was. One of the chaps I was with couldn't get over it. Welsh fellow, always going on about it. "Just like dandelions, Sun-Up, wasn't it?" he said to me. "Walking along, and you take a swing at a line of dandelion clocks with a stick or something, and you think, if I'm really clever I can knock them off and have them float down without disturbing the feathers." That's what he thought.

'The ones that haunt you . . . they aren't really the ones you expect. I've had mates shot down only a few yards away. I've seen them get into a spin, I've shouted at them over the R/T, I've known they couldn't bale out and followed them down and seen them go, and thought, I hope someone sees me off like this when it's my turn. It shakes you at the time, and for a bit afterwards, but it doesn't haunt you. The ones that haunt you are where there's no fucking dignity. Sorry. I'm going to get it, you think, and sometimes you almost get used to the idea; but you still want it on your own terms. It shouldn't matter, but it does. It really does.

'I heard about some poor blighter at Castle Bromwich. He was testing a Spitfire. Took off, pointed the nose up, and started climbing as hard as he could. Got up to about fifteen thou, something went wrong. Came right back down again: from fifteen thou straight into the tarmac he'd taken off from. They had to dig down quite a way. Then they had to have what was left of him looked at in case it was carbon monoxide in the oxygen supply or something, so they collected what they could find and sent it off for analysis. They sent it off in a *sweet jar*.' He paused. 'That's what matters.'

Jean couldn't really follow his horror. Dandelion clocks, sweet jars — of course it sounded undignified. Perhaps because it sounded homely, not grand enough. But there wasn't anything very pretty or dignified about getting shot down or diving into a hillside or being burnt alive in your cockpit. Perhaps she was too young to understand about death and its superstitions.

'So what's the best way to . . . get it?'

'I used to think about that all the time. All the time. When the whole thing started I used to see myself somewhere near Dover. Sunshine, seagulls, the old white cliffs gleaming away — real Vera Lynn stuff. Anyway, there I'd be, no ammo, not much juice left, and suddenly a whole squadron of Heinkels comes along. Like a great swarm of flies. I'd intercept, get right in

28

among them, fuselage like a colander, then I'd pick out the leader of the battle group, fly straight at him and smash into his tail. We'd both go down together. Very romantic.'

'It sounds very brave.'

'No, it's not brave. It's pretty stupid, and anyway it's wasteful. One of theirs for one of ours isn't a good enough ratio.'

'So what about now?' Jean half-surprised herself with her question.

'Oh, now. It's a bit more realistic. And a bit more wasteful. Now I'd like to get it the way quite a few pilots — the young ones, especially — used to get it back in '39, '40.

'That's one of the funny things you notice. You can't get better without experience, but it's while you're getting the experience that you're most likely to get knocked down. It's always the youngest chaps that you might not see again at the end of an op. So as the war goes on, what happens in a squadron is that the old get older and the young get younger. Then some of the old ones get pulled out because they're too valuable to lose, and you end up less experienced than you started off.

'Anyway. Imagine you're up there, really high. When you get over 25,000 it's like a different world. Very cold for a start; and the aeroplane handles differently. It climbs slower and it skids around the sky because the air's so thin and the props don't have enough to bite on, and everything slips a bit as you try to control it. Then your Perspex starts misting over and you can't see too well.

'You haven't been on many ops and you've had a bit of a scare and you're climbing. You're climbing straight into the sun because you think that's safe. It's all much brighter than usual up there. You hold your hand up in front of your face and you open your fingers very slightly and squint through them. You carry on climbing. You stare through your fingers at the sun, and you notice that the nearer you get to it, the colder you feel. You ought to worry about this but you don't. You don't because you're happy.

'The reason you're happy is you've got a small oxygen leak.

You don't suspect anything's wrong; your reactions are slower, but you think they're normal. Then you get a bit feebler; you don't move your head around as much as you should. You aren't in pain, you don't even feel the cold now. You don't want to kill anyone any more — all that feeling has been leaking away with the oxygen. You feel *happy*.

'And then one of two things happens. Either a 109 drops on you with a quick burst and a whouf of flame and then it's all over, nice and clean. Or else, nothing at all happens, and you carry on climbing through the thin blue air, staring at the sun through your fingers, frost on your Perspex but all warm inside, all happy and not a thought in your head, until your hand drops in front of you, and then your head drops, and you don't even notice it's curtains . . . '

What possible answer could you make to that, Jean thought. You couldn't shout 'Don't do it!' as if Prosser were a suicide on a parapet. You couldn't very well say it all sounded brave and beautiful to you, even if that was exactly what it did sound like. You just had to wait for him to say the next thing.

'Sometimes I think they oughtn't to let me back to flying. I can see myself doing that one day. When I've had enough. Have to do it over the sea, of course, otherwise you might land in someone's allotment. Might stop them Digging for Victory.'

'That wouldn't do.'

'No, that wouldn't do at all.'

'And . . . and you haven't had enough.' Jean intended this as a gentle question, but she seemed to panic half-way through and it came out bossy and certain. Prosser's tone hardened in reply.

'Well, you're a good listener little missie, aren't you, but you don't know the first thing. You don't know the first thing.'

'At least I know that I don't,' Jean said, rather to her surprise; and to his, for the sting went out of his tone at once. He carried on, in a sort of reverie.

'It really is quite different up there, you see. I mean, when you've flown as much as I have, you find you can suddenly get completely browned-off, just in a minute or so. Something to do with nerves, I suppose — you've been tense for so long, and then if you relax a bit, it feels like for ever. You should talk to some of those flying-boat chappies if you want to hear funny stories.'

Did she want to hear funny stories? Not if they were about sweet jars and dandelion clocks; but Prosser didn't give her the chance to say no.

'Chum of mine, he was on Catalinas. They can be on duty twenty, twenty-two hours at a stretch. Up at midnight, breakfast, take-off two in the morning, not back till eight or nine at night. Flying over the same bit of sea for hours on end: that's what it feels like. Not even steering — they've handed over to George most of the time. Just staring at the sea, looking for subs and waiting for the next brew-up. That's when your eyes start playing tricks. This chum of mine said he was once out in the Atlantic, nothing much happening, when suddenly he pulled the stick right back. Thought there was a mountain ahead.'

'Perhaps it was one of those clouds that looks like a mountain.'

'No. After he'd flattened out and they'd all effed him for spilling their brew-up, he had a good look round. Nothing, not a cloud in the sky, absolutely clear . . . And then, another bloke I talked to, he had it even odder. Guess what? He was four hundred and fifty miles off the west coast of Ireland, tooling along, he looks down, and what does he see? He sees a fellow on a motor-bike, riding along like it was Sunday afternoon.'

'In the air?'

'Course not. Don't be daft. You can't ride along in the air. No, he was obeying the traffic regulations and going along in a straight line on the top of the waves. Goggles, leather gauntlets, exhaust smoke coming out the back. Looking as happy as Larry.'

Jean giggled. 'Riding on the water. Like Jesus.'

'None of that if you please,' said Prosser disapprovingly. 'I'm not that way inclined, but don't blaspheme in front of those who are going to get it.'

'I'm sorry.'

'Granted.'

*　　*　　*　　*

'Who are you?'

'I'm a policeman.'

'Are you really?'

'Yes.'

'Really really? You don't look like a policeman.'

'We have to be masters of disguise, miss.'

'But if you disguise yourself too well no one will know that you're a policeman.'

'You can always tell.'

'How?'

'Come a bit closer and I'll show you.'

He was standing by the creosoted front gate with the sunrise motif cut into its top half; she was in the middle of the concrete path, on her way to feel the washing. He was a tall man, with a fleshy head and a schoolboy's neck; he stood awkwardly, his brown herringbone overcoat reaching almost to his ankles.

'The feet,' he said, pointing downwards. She looked. No, they weren't enormous great flatfeet; they were quite small, actually. But there was something a bit funny about them ... Were they the wrong way round? Yes, that was it — both his feet were pointing outwards.

'Did you put your shoes on the wrong way round?' she asked, a bit obviously.

'Certainly not, miss. That's the way every policeman's feet are. It's in the regulations.' She still almost believed him. 'Some of the recruits', he added, in a voice that spoke of wet dungeons, 'have to have *operations*.' Now she didn't believe him. She laughed, and then again as he stagily uncrossed his legs beneath the engulfing overcoat and set them down the right way round.

'Have you come to arrest me?'

'I've come about the blackout.'

Looking back, she thought it was an odd way to meet a

husband. But no odder than some, she supposed. And compared to others, almost quite promising.

He called again about the blackout. The third time he just happened to be passing.

'Would you like to come to the pub a hop the tea-shop out for a walk out for a drive out to meet my parents?'

She laughed. 'I expect one of them will be all right with Mother.'

One of them was, and they took to meeting. She found that his eyes were dark brown, that he was tall and a bit unpredictable; but mostly tall. He found her tentative, trusting and guileless to the point of rebuke.

'Can't you put sugar in it?' she asked after tasting her first half of mild and bitter.

'I'm sorry,' he replied, 'I completely forgot. I'll get you something else instead.' The next time, he ordered her another half of mild and bitter, then passed her a screw of paper. She tipped the sugar in and screamed as the beer fizzed out of the glass; it poured towards her, making her jump off her stool.

'Never fails to amuse, does it, sir?' said the publican as he swabbed down the bar. Michael laughed. Jean felt embarrassed. He thought she was stupid, didn't he? The man who ran the pub certainly thought she was stupid.

'Do you know how many sandwiches Lindbergh took with him when he crossed the Atlantic?'

Michael was taken aback, as much by the sudden tone of authority as by the question. Perhaps it was a riddle. That must be it; so he dutifully replied, 'I don't know. How many sandwiches *did* Lindbergh take with him when he flew the Atlantic?'

'Five,' she said emphatically, 'but he only ate one and a half.'

'Oh,' was all he could think of saying.

'Why do you think he only ate one and a half?' she asked.

Maybe it was a riddle after all. 'I don't know. Why *did* he only eat one and a half?'

'I don't know.'

'Oh.'

'I thought you might know,' she said disappointedly.

'Perhaps he only ate one and a half because they came from the ABC and were stale.' They both laughed, mainly out of gratitude that the conversation hadn't entirely gurgled away.

Very quickly Jean supposed that she loved him. She must, mustn't she? She thought about him all the time; she lay awake and dreamed all kinds of fancies; she liked to look at his face, which struck her as full and interesting and wise, not at all fleshy as she'd first imagined, and those patches of red that flared in his cheeks showed character; she was slightly afraid of displeasing him; and she judged him to be the sort of man who would look after her. If that wasn't love, what was?

One evening he walked her home under a high, calm sky, a sky empty of clouds and aeroplanes. He sang softly, as if to himself, in the placeless American accent of an international crooner:

> Heads we marry, honey,
> Tails we take a cruise;
> Heads it is so tell your people the news . . .

Then he just hummed the tune, and she imagined the words repeated. That was all, until they got back to the creosoted gate with the cut-out sunrise, where Jean pressed herself hard into the lapel of his jacket before breaking away and running inside. Maybe it was some awful tease, she thought, like one of Uncle Leslie's pranks. She hummed the tune to herself as if to find out, but it was no real help; it was just a wonderful tune.

The next evening, when they reached the same point in the lane and the sky proved just as tender, she found herself almost panting. Without breaking his stride, Michael resumed the story:

> Heads we have six children,
> Tails we keep a cat;
> Heads it is so whaddya know about that . . .

She didn't know what to say. She couldn't think straight at all.

'Michael, I've something to ask.'

'Yes?' They both stopped.

'When you first came along that day ... There wasn't anything wrong with our blackout, was there?'

'No.'

'I thought there wasn't. And then you told me those fibs about policemen's feet.'

'Guilty as charged.'

'*And* you didn't tell me you didn't put sugar in beer.'

'No ma'am.'

'So why should I marry someone like that?'

She stopped. He put his arm through hers while thinking of an answer. 'Well, if I'd called at your house and said, "I'd just like to tell you your blackout curtains fit perfectly and by the way my feet are the right way round if you'd care to inspect them," you wouldn't have looked at me twice.'

'I might not have.' He put his arms around her. 'And I've something else to ask while we're sorting things out.' He moved forward slightly as if preparing to kiss her, but she persevered. It was only one of childhood's questions, but she distantly felt that they ought all to be settled before her adult life began. 'Why is the mink tenacious of life?'

'Is that another riddle?'

'No. I just want to know.'

'Why is the mink tenacious of life? What a funny question.' They walked on; he assumed that she didn't want to be kissed yet. 'They're nasty, vicious little things, minks,' he announced, not entirely happy with this answer.

'Is that why they're tenacious of life?'

'Probably. Nasty vicious little things usually do fight for their lives more than big soft things.'

'Hmm.' It wasn't quite the answer she'd been hoping for. She'd expected something more specific. But that would do for the moment. They walked on. Glancing at the sky, which was high and serene, with just a scatter of light, loose evening clouds, she said,

'Well, when are we getting married, then?'

He smiled, nodded, and quietly hummed his tune.

It must be right to love Michael. Or, if it wasn't right, she must love him. Or, even if she didn't love him, she must marry him. No, no, of course she loved him, and of course it was right. Michael was the answer, whatever might have been the question.

She hadn't had many suitors, but didn't mind. Suitor was such a silly word that the men who were suitors must be silly too. 'He pressed his suit.' She had heard that phrase somewhere, or read it, and it always struck her that this was what was wrong with suitors. Were they called suitors because they were always pressing their suits? She liked men smart, but she didn't like them spivvy.

In her head she lined up for comparison the men she knew. Perhaps men could be divided into suitors and husbands. Leslie and Tommy Prosser were probably good at being suitors, but it might be a mistake to marry them. They were a bit raffish, and their explanations of the world might not be reliable. Whereas Father and Michael were probably good at being husbands; they didn't look spivvy, and kept their feet on the ground. Yes, that was another way of looking at it: men either had their feet on the ground or their heads in the air. Michael, the first time she had met him, had drawn attention to his feet; they were pointing the wrong way, but they were firmly on the ground.

Judged by this new criterion, the four men she knew still divided up in the same way. Suddenly, she pictured herself kissing Tommy Prosser, and the thought of his moustache made her shudder: she had practised once on a toothbrush, and it had confirmed her vividest fears. Michael was taller than any of them, and had Prospects of Promotion, a phrase to which her mother always awarded capital letters. He was, Jean admitted, a little shabby beneath his engulfing overcoat, but after the war she could smarten him up. That was what women did in marriage, wasn't it? They rescued men from their failings and vices. Yes, she thought, smiling: *I* shall press *his* suit.

And that seemed to be it. If this wasn't love, what was? And

36

did he love her? Of course. He said so every time they kissed goodnight. Father said you can always trust a policeman.

There was one subject on which Michael got ratty: that of Tommy Prosser. Perhaps it was her fault. She did rather go on about Tommy, but that was natural, wasn't it? She was at home all day; Tommy was around some of the time; and when Michael came to collect her and asked what she'd been doing, well, it wasn't very interesting to go on about blacking the grate and hanging out the washing, was it? So Jean would tell him what Tommy Prosser had said. Once she asked him if he knew what an All Clear sandwich was.

'You're always asking me about sandwiches,' said Michael. '*Sandwiches*.'

'It's got dandelions in it.'

'Sounds utterly disgusting.'

'It wasn't very nice.'

'He's shifty, that's what I don't like about him. Doesn't look you in the eye. Always turning his head away. I like a man who looks you in the eye.'

'He's not as tall as you.'

'What's that got to do with it, stupid?'

'Well, maybe that's why he doesn't look you in the eye.'

'That's got nothing to do with it.'

Oh well. Probably it was a good idea not to tell Michael that Prosser was grounded, even though you shouldn't have any secrets from your husband. She didn't say that he was called Sun-Up either.

Prosser didn't get ratty when she talked about Michael; though he didn't always join in her enthusiasm.

'He'll do all right,' was his standard reply.

'You do think it's a good idea, don't you, Tommy?'

'Good enough, lass. I'll tell you this, he's got a good bargain.'

'But you're married? And you're happy?'

'Haven't been home enough to notice.'

'No, I suppose not. But you do like Michael?'

'He'll do all right. It's not me that's marrying him.'

'Isn't he tall?'

'He's tall enough.'

'But you do think he'll make a wonderful husband?'

'You've got to get burned once. Just try not to get burned twice.' She didn't really understand this remark, but she was rather cross with Tommy Prosser about it anyway.

* * * *

Mrs Barrett, one of the brisker, more modern wives of the village, called on Jean when everyone was out of the house and gave her a small parcel. '*I* don't need it any longer, my dear,' was all she said. Later, in bed, Jean unwrapped a maroon cloth-bound book of advice designed for young couples. At the front was a list of the author's previous works. She had written *The Cretaceous Flora* (in two parts), *Ancient Plants, The Study of Plant Life, A Journal from Japan*, a three-act play called *Our Ostriches* and a dozen books under the heading Sexology. One of these was called *The First Five Thousand*. The first five thousand *what*?

Jean wasn't sure how to read the book, or whether she should be doing so anyway. Wasn't it better to learn such things from Michael? He was bound to know most of this, wasn't he? Or was he? It wasn't an area they had discussed. Men were supposed to know, and women were supposed not to mind how they had found out. Jean didn't mind: it was silly to worry about Michael's life before she met him. It seemed so distant anyway — it was all before the war. The word *prostitute* sidled into her mind like a vamp through a door. Men went to prostitutes to rid themselves of their animal desires, then later they married wives — that was what happened, wasn't it? Did you have to go to London for prostitutes? She supposed so. Most of the unpleasant things to do with sex took place, she imagined, in London.

The first night she leafed through the book carelessly, skipping whole chapters called Sleep, Children, Society, and Appendix. If she did this, it didn't really count as reading. Even so, phrases dropped from the page and stuck like burrs to her winceyette nightdress. Some of them made her laugh; some of them made her apprehensive. The word *turgid* kept appearing, as did *crisis*; she didn't like the sound of those two. *Enlarged and stiffened*, she read; *lubricated by mucus*; *turgid* again; *soft, small and drooping* (ugh); *maladjustment of the relative shapes and positions of the organs*; *partial absorption of the man's secretions*; *congestion of the womb*.

At the back of the book was an advertisement for the author's play, the one called *Our Ostriches*, 'first produced at the Royal Court Theatre Nov. 14 1923'. *Punch* said it was 'full of humour and irony, admirably interpreted'. The *Sunday Times* said it 'begins in excitement and keeps it up all through'. Jean found herself giggling, and became suddenly shocked at herself. What a dirty mind. But then she giggled again as she imagined another review that read: 'admirably turgid'.

She told Michael that Mrs Barrett had given her the book. 'Good show,' he said, looking away. 'I'd been wondering about all that.'

She thought of asking him about prostitutes, but they were approaching that part of the lane where he hummed, and she decided this wasn't the best time. Still, he clearly thought it was a good idea that she was reading the book; so that night she went back to it more purposefully. She was astonished by how often the word *sex* seemed to be married to some other word: *sex-attraction*, *sex-ignorance*, *sex-tide*, *sex-life*, *sex-function*. Lots of hyphens everywhere. Sex–hyphens, she thought.

She tried hard, but couldn't understand a lot of what was being said. The author made great claims to write plainly and straightforwardly, but Jean got lost almost at once. *Soul structures*, she read, and *the rift within the lute*, which she didn't much want to think about. *The clitoris corresponds morphologically to the man's penis*. What could that mean? And there weren't many jokes around. *The Queen of Aragon ordained that six times a day was the proper rule in legitimate marriage. So abnormally sexed a woman would to-day probably succeed in killing by exhaustion a succession of husbands* . . . that was the nearest.

Even the parts which she could understand without difficulty didn't seem to correspond to her experience. *The opportunities for peaceful, romantic dalliance*, she read, *are less to-day in a city with its tubes and cinema-shows than in woods and gardens where the pulling of rosemary or lavender may be the sweet excuse for the slow and profound mutual rousing of passion*. Admittedly it was wartime, but Michael and she might as well live in the city for all the pulling of lavender he had proposed. She couldn't offhand think of where it might grow locally. And why was it herbs that were suggested? What was wrong with flowers?

Then there was something called the Periodicity of Recurrence, a sort of graph showing how a woman's desire came and went through the month. There were two charts, one showing the Curve of Normal Desire in Healthy Women, the second showing the Feeble and Transient Up-Welling in Women Suffering from Fatigue and Overwork. At the end of the second graph the Level of Potential Desire suddenly shot up and down like a ping-pong ball on a water-fountain. A caption explained: 'Shortly before and during the time of the crest *d* Alpine air restored the vitality of the subject.'

Finally, there was a piece of advice she noted in the section called Modesty and Romance. *Be always escaping. Escape the lower, the trivial, the sordid. So far as possible ensure that you allow your husband to come upon you only when there is delight in the meeting. Whenever the finances allow, the husband and wife should have separate bedrooms, failing that they should have a curtain which can at will be drawn so as to divide the room they share.*

When she next saw Michael she had three questions.

'What does *morphologically* mean?'

'Give up. Anything to do with sandwiches?'

'And do you ever want to go out and look for lavender and rosemary?'

He glanced across at her a bit more seriously. 'Is the wind blowing from the Colney Hatch or something?'

'And can we have separate rooms?'

'Isn't this a bit sudden? I haven't laid a finger on you yet, darling.'

'But you're supposed to be the hunter who ever dreams of coming unawares upon Diana in the woodlands.'

'Gathering lavender and rosemary?'

'I suppose so.'

'Then I'd better go get me a hoss.' They laughed together, then Michael added, 'And in any case, why should I want Diana in the woodlands when I've got Jean by the front hedge?'

That night, she put away the book. It was clearly rubbish. Three days later, Michael said casually, 'Oh, by the way, I've made an appointment for you.'

'Who with?'

'In London. She's very nice, apparently. So they tell me.'

'She's . . . not a dentist?'

'No.' He looked away. 'She'll . . . sort of inspect you.'

'Do I need inspecting?' Jean felt surprised rather than offended. Presumably everyone had to be inspected. 'Will you send me back if I'm defective?'

'No, no, of course not, darling.' He took her hand. 'It's just something that . . . women have to do. I mean, nowadays, they do.'

'I've never heard of anyone being sent off to London to get inspected,' said Jean rather crossly. What had country people done before the railways?

'Oh, it's not that, darling, not just that. It's . . . things like babies.'

It was her turn to look away. Oh dear, she thought. But didn't men take the responsibility for that? Isn't that what *responsibility* meant in the book? Suddenly, she thought of other words; *turgid*, and *the rift within the lute*, and *lubricated by mucus*. The whole thing seemed an awful idea.

'Can't we just be friends?' she asked.

'We *are* friends now. That's why we're getting married. When we're married we'll still be friends; but we'll be . . . married. That's what it's about.'

'I see.' She didn't really. She felt miserable.

'Will you take me off for some Alpine air if I'm defective?' she asked.

'Just as soon as Private Hitler allows,' he promised. 'Just as soon as Private Hitler allows.'

Dr Headley would have made an excellent dentist, Jean thought. She was bright in manner, professional, informative, articulate, friendly and utterly frightening. She wore a white coat open over a suit which might as well have been a uniform. She sat Jean on a couch and relaxed her with small-talk about the Blitz. It seemed the wrong way round to Jean, who suddenly said, 'I've come to be inspected.'

'Of course you have. We'll do the inspection today and the fitting next week. I find most girls don't like to rush things.'

'I see.' What fitting? Oh dear.

Dr Headley then asked questions about Jean and Michael, some of which seemed very circumstantial.

'And what do you know about the sexual act? Tell me frankly.' Jean mentioned the book in the maroon cloth binding, the one by the woman whose play about ostriches began in excitement and kept it up all through. 'Splendid. So you must know most of it by now. Always best to get some reading under your belt. And what do you think of the sexual act — I mean, about it generally?'

By now Jean had more confidence. Nothing would shock Dr Headley. Her hair was swept off her face and piled into a neat but lopsided bun; Jean was reminded of a cottage loaf.

'I think it's funny.'

'Funny? You mean strange. Yes, it can be at first. But you get used to it.'

'No, funny. Funny-ha-ha. Funny-ha-ha.' *Turgid*, she thought; *rift in the lute*; *lavender*; *the Queen of Aragon*. She allowed herself to giggle.

'Funny, my girl, is the one thing it is not.' Oh dear. 'It is intensely serious. It is beautiful, and it can be complicated, but it is *not funny*. Do you see?' Jean nodded, blushing at her gaffe, yet still only half-convinced. 'Now slip behind that screen and

42

take off your nether garments.'

Chastened, Jean did so. She wondered about her shoes. Were shoes garments? Should she put them back on? Oh dear. She should never have said that sex was funny. Of course, it could well turn out not to be. Perhaps her Periodicity of Recurrence would astonish her; perhaps she wouldn't need any Alpine air. She tried not to, but she couldn't help thinking about Michael's penis. Not the thing itself, which she had yet to imagine, let alone see; but the idea of it. The thing that would join their bodies together — the sex-hyphen.

She came out from behind the screen. She was asked to lie down, and then ... oh dear. Wild horses, she thought. The silence was terrible. Jean began to hum quietly to herself. 'Heads we marry, honey ... ' Then she stopped in embarrassment. Dr Headley probably disapproved of humming, even if the tune was appropriate.

'This may feel a little cold.' Jean braced herself. Was she going to be doused with cold water, as punishment for her levity in humming? But no: it was only ... she stopped thinking about her nether regions. Her eyes were tight shut, like blackout curtains closely drawn; but through them came the red glow of life outside. Black and red, the colour of the war: the colour of Tommy Prosser's war. Tommy Prosser in his black Hurricane out in the black night with the hood back and the red glow from the instrument panel softly lighting up his face and hands. Tommy Prosser in his black Hurricane looking out for the red exhausts of returning bombers. Black and red ...

'Well, the nursery's fine, and there's nothing wrong with the playroom,' said Dr Headley all of a sudden.

'Oh good.' What was she talking about?

Dr Headley pulled open a drawer and extracted three circular tins with numbers written on them. She put away the two larger ones with a jovial, 'Mustn't frighten the horses,' and opened the third. A haze of French chalk rose as she unscrewed the lid. 'Now I'll just show you the principle of the thing, and next week you can try it for yourself.'

43

Dr Headley extracted the Dutch cap and tapped the chalk off it. 'Quite simple, see? Spring round there' — she compressed the cap into a slim figure of eight — 'flexible, tough, completely safe if you put it in right, you try.'

Jean picked it up. It looked enormous. Where did it go? Perhaps you wrapped it round the sex-hyphen like a piece of groundsheet and lashed it down with rope. Tentatively, she squeezed the edges of the thing. It seemed quite resistant. Then she laid it flat on the blotter in front of her and tried again. The spring yielded, and a fold of black rubber came bellying up into the palm of her hand. She squealed.

'You'll soon get used to it.' Jean had her doubts. Anything for Michael, of course; but couldn't they just be friends? 'Now this is the lubricating jelly.' Dr Headley suddenly had a tube in her hand. Oh dear. What had happened to *lubricated by mucus*?

'Don't . . . is that . . . necessary?'

Dr Headley gave a chuckle, and didn't bother to answer.

'I thought you said it wasn't funny?' Jean felt cross with this woman she had been lured to see.

'No, I wasn't laughing at it. I was laughing at you. You girls always want it both ways; all the pleasure and none of the responsibility.' As she said that word *responsibility*, she began to smear some jelly round the cap's rim, then into the soft central hammock of rubber. A brief demonstration, then she passed it over. 'No, grasp it firmly, it won't bite. No, more firmly. Thumb and fingers, thumb and fingers, haven't you ever done glove puppets?'

Jean put it down before it squirted out of control. That was surely enough for today.

At Paddington, waiting for her train, Jean found a heavy, green-painted machine with a large clock-face. In place of the hours there were letters of the alphabet. You turned a big metal pointer, and for a penny could print fifteen letters on to a thin strip of tin. A chipped enamel plate suggested that you might like to send a message to a friend by this means. Jean didn't think she had any messages to send. She didn't have the confidence for self-pity; she felt merely forlorn. Laboriously, she moved the metal pointer among the letters, pressed a handle, and printed out JEAN, followed by SERJEANT. That left her with three spare letters; Father, even though he probably considered such expenditure frivolous, would have wanted her to get her money's worth. Name, rank and number, that was the phrase, wasn't it? Jean didn't have a rank, nor did she own a number. After a little thought, she printed XXX, extracted her tin strip from the side of the machine, and put it in her handbag.

*　*　*　*

Jean assumed, rather vaguely, that something must have happened to Tommy Prosser in the last year; something specific and identifiable. Before, he had been a brave Hurricane pilot, now he was grounded, ratty and frightened. All she had to do was locate the source of this fear, allow him to talk about some dreadful, scarring incident that had taken place, and he would be on the mend. This much Jean understood of psychoanalytic principle.

One afternoon, she sat at the kitchen table with a tin of Silvo and the forks drawn up before her like soldiery. Prosser sounded less belligerent than usual. He began talking of 1940 as if it were Mons or Ypres: something distant that hadn't happened to him.

'The first time I put the wind up myself, it was real music-hall. I was having a bit of an argument with a couple of 109s over the North Sea. It wasn't turning out to be a good idea, so I ran for some cloud, dodged around a bit and headed back to base. Fast as I could. You dive when you want to go fast, you see. Anyway, there I was, and suddenly, machine-guns. One of the 109s must have followed me down. I hauled the stick back quick as a flash and went into a big, looping turn. Had a good look round, but couldn't see anything. Must have shaken him off.

'So, nose down for base again. Faster and faster. Then, guess what, more guns. I haul the stick back and just as I do the firing stops. I was climbing hard and looking for cloud when it suddenly dawned on me. I was fair bumping along in the dive and I must have been gripping the stick tighter and tighter. The button's on top of the stick, you see. So what I was doing was setting off my own guns and scaring myself silly. Wheeling about the sky like a proper Charlie.'

Jean smiled. 'Did you tell them when you got back?'

'No. Not at first. Not until someone else admitted a bigger goof. And then they thought I was shooting a line.'

'Do people always own up when things go wrong?'

'Course not.'

'What didn't you own up to?'

'What didn't we own up to? The usual things. Getting scared. Getting scared of letting chaps down. Thinking you wouldn't come back. Mind you, you could always tell the signs, when someone was thinking about not coming back. You'd be sitting in the dispersal hut, and you'd notice someone being polite. I mean, really polite, all of a sudden. And you'd realize he'd been like that for a couple of days, always passing the sugar, talking quietly, not putting anyone's back up. All the time thinking about not coming back. Wants to be remembered as a nice chap. Doesn't know he's doing it, of course — hasn't the foggiest idea.'

'Did you get like that?'

'How would I know? You don't know you're doing it. Maybe I was doing something else — rattling the pennies in my pocket or something.'

'You aren't allowed to admit you're scared?'

'Course not. Bad form. Even if you know the other chaps can tell.'

'Can I ask you something?'

'You already have, haven't you?' Prosser flicked a smile at her, as if to say, Yes, I am in a better mood today. Jean looked down: it was like being caught rattling the pennies in her pocket. 'Fire away.'

'Well, I wondered what it was like being brave.'

'Being *brave*?' This wasn't what Prosser had expected. 'What do you want to know that for?'

'I'm interested. I mean, it's all right if . . . '

46

'No . . . it's . . . just that it's difficult. I mean, it varies. You can do something normal and the other chaps decide you've been brave; or you can think you've put up quite a good show and they don't even mention it.'

'So who decides what being brave is? Them or you?'

'I don't know. I suppose you do in a way, but they do when it comes to gongs and so on. You don't really think about it that way round, you see.'

'Now you're being modest.' Jean had noticed the ribbons on Sun-Up Prosser's uniform. You didn't get them for nothing.

'No, no. I'm not. I mean, you don't decide, "Now I'm going to be brave", or sit back afterwards and think, "Gosh, that was brave".'

'But you must make some decision. If you see someone's in trouble and you say, "I'm going to help him".'

'No. You say much less printable things than that. And then you do it. It's not like making a decision in civvy life. It's whouf, and you're in it. Sometimes things are a bit clearer and you've got time to think, but what you think is what you've been trained to think in the circs, and sometimes it's a bit hazy as if you're whistled, but mostly it's whouf, there you are.'

'Oh.'

'Sorry to disappoint. It may be different for others. I can't tell you what it's like being brave. You can't pick it up and look at it. When it's there you don't feel it's there. You don't feel excited or dizzy or something. Maybe you feel a bit more as if you know what you're doing, but that's the limit. You can't talk about it. It isn't there.' Prosser began to sound a bit het-up. 'I mean, it isn't the sensible thing, is it? The sensible thing is to be so scared your pants are falling off. That's the *sensible* reaction.'

'And is that different? I mean, is that like having something, being frightened?'

'Ah, *fear*. Yes, that's quite different.' He seemed to calm down as quickly as he had heated up. 'Quite different. You want to know about that?'

'Yes please.' Jean suddenly became aware of how different

talking to Prosser was from talking to Michael. It was harder in some ways, but . . .

'Number one, you know when you've got it. Number two, everyone else does as well. Number three, you know what it's making you do while you're doing it.'

'What does it make you do?'

'Makes you do everything. Not very much at first. You look in the mirror a bit more. Fly a bit higher or a bit lower than's necessary. Get the safety bug. Break off a scrap a bit earlier than you normally would. Shoot a line or two in the mess. Find a few more things going wrong with the aeroplane than you did before. Little things that make you turn back a bit earlier, or make you lose touch with your formation.

'Then comes the bit when you start to notice it. Probably because you notice other people noticing it. You get back and the ground crew do what they always do — look to see if the guns have been fired before you're out of the cockpit. And if they haven't been fired a couple of times in a row, you imagine them muttering a bit. Always the same word, you imagine. *Windy.* Windy. So you think, I'm not having them calling me windy, so what you might start doing is drift off from your formation, get into a bit of cloud and fire your guns. If you fire them long enough you run out of ammo and have to make for home anyway. And you give your ground crew the thumb as you taxi in, and tell them you're pretty sure about a Heinkel — it was smoking pretty badly and while you didn't see it go down you thought if they did get back to Germany it would be on Shanks's pony — and they give a cheer and you half-believe it yourself and wonder whether to mention it at debriefing, and you realize you have to because what if you were boasting about hits to your ground crew and not mentioning them to Intelligence, and someone found out? So you do, and before you know where you are you've knocked down the whole bloody Luftwaffe who must have been flying through that load of cloud you fired your guns into.'

'Is that what you did?'

'That's how it ended up the second time, when they posted me. The first time there were a few little signs, I wasn't sure, they weren't sure, so they took me off flying orders for a few days. But I knew when it happened the second time. Then I knew what the first time was.'

'It was probably just nerves the first time.'

'Yes, that's just what it was. Nerves, being scared, windy, yellow, exactly. You know what they say, don't you? A man burnt twice is finished.' Jean remembered that was the phrase he had used when she'd asked him about marrying Michael.

'I'm sure that's an old wives' tale.'

'Old wives know a thing or two.' He chuckled. 'Ask mine.'

'Tell me what it's like, being scared.'

'I've told you what it's like. It's running away. It's being windy.'

'But what's it like inside?'

Prosser pondered. He knew exactly what it felt like. He dreamed about what it felt like.

'Well, some parts of it are like other things. Like trembling hands and a dry mouth and tense in the head — that's all part of good healthy nerves before an op. Usually. Sometimes it isn't. Normally you get these little signs in the dispersal hut, then when you're off the ground they go away; then they might come back when there looks like being some action, but when you get close they go away again. Except that sometimes they're there all the time, even when you're coming back safely, and that's a bad sign. And then you start to get the fear.'

He paused, and looked across at Jean. She held his gaze as he went on.

'Imagine swallowing something sour, like vinegar. Imagine you don't just taste it in your mouth, but all the way down. Imagine you can taste it in your mouth, in your gullet, in your chest, in your stomach. Then imagine that it's all congealing very slowly between your chest and your throat. Slowly congealing. Porridge made of vinegar, tasting everywhere. Sour in your mouth. Wet and slack in your stomach. Congealing like porridge between your throat and your chest. That means you can't trust your voice. So sometimes you pretend the R/T has broken down; sometimes you pretend to be going through a strong silent patch. You keep your mouth shut and you let the sourness bump against your throat. Half your body is full of this sour sick, and because you can taste it all the time you think you can sick it up and get rid of it. But you can't. It just stays there, cold and sour and congealing, and you know there's no good reason for it ever to go away. Ever. Because it's quite right to be there.'

'It might go away,' she said, conscious of a false brightness in her voice; as if she'd patted an amputee and assured him his legs would start growing again soon.

'Twice burnt,' he replied quietly.

'I'm sure you can get it back,' she went on, her voice still full of district nurse. 'Back to poaching over the dromes and things . . . whatever.'

'That was before,' said Prosser. 'That was when everyone was doing khaki knitting wherever you looked. Remember?'

'I've still got mine. I never quite finished it.'

'That was it. Khaki knitting. Hate the Hun. Repel the invader. It was all nice and clear and you were happy. You thought you might die, but that didn't seem so important; and you didn't think how long it was going to last or anything, you just got on with it. And anyway it was all new. And bits of it were like the best bits of your life.'

'Like watching the sun rise twice.'

'Like watching the sun rise twice. Like taking some bombers across to their target and getting there and the reception committee throwing up a lot of dirt, and you just looked at it — green and yellow and red, hanging in the air — and you didn't think about it hurting you, you thought about how it looked like paper streamers at a Saturday night hop. Now it's different. You can't go on like that forever.'

'And you don't hate the Germans as much as you used to?' Jean thought they were getting somewhere. Perhaps courage comes from hatred, or at least is kept going by it. Sun-Up had lost his hate, that was all. Nothing shameful about this; quite the contrary.

'No, no. I hate them just as much. Just exactly as much. Maybe for different reasons, but just exactly as much.'

'Oh. Did ... did something happen? Something awful?' Something which made you not brave any more.

Prosser smiled carefully, as if he really would make things simple for her if he could. It was just that he couldn't.

'Sorry. It's not like that. The boy grows to manhood overnight. The man becomes a hero. The hero cracks. New boys arrive, new heroes are welded.' He was almost teasing her, though not in a way she'd ever been teased before. 'It's not like that. I didn't crack — at least, not how everyone thinks of it. Things just run out after a while. The stocks are exhausted. There isn't anything left. People tell you it's just a question of having a break and recharging the batteries. But there are a lot of batteries that won't recharge. Or not any more.'

'Don't be so pessimistic,' she said, though she felt unconvinced by her cheerful voice. 'You still love flying, don't you?'

'I still love flying.'

'And you still hate the Germans?'

'I still hate the Germans.'

'Well then, Mr Prosser?'

'Well then Mrs soon-to-be Michael Curtis, I'm afraid you haven't got a QED there.'

'Oh. Oh, but I'm sure. I just know it. Think of the sunrises.'

'Well,' said Prosser, 'I'm not sure I want to any more. You see the sun rise twice — you get burned twice. That seems fair enough to me. Fair dos. Just better get used to it. May as well sling my hook.'

'No, please don't get used to it.'

'I wasn't serious.'

* * * *

The following week Jean returned to see Dr Headley. She made herself promise not to find anything funny. Not that there was much likelihood of this.

The circular tin came out again, and the French chalk rose, and the smearing of the jelly was demonstrated, and again Jean thought, *lubricated by mucus*? Perhaps it was a tube of mucus-jelly. Then she was upended, as if she'd chosen the wrong machine at a funfair, and ordered to relax. She relaxed by floating, then flying away from what was happening to her. She was in a black Hurricane and the clouds were streaming past. Sun-Up Prosser had had a wicker seat installed in his cockpit, and was taking her for a ride; it wasn't just whooping cough, he said, that could be cured by flight. And he would show her his trick. Uncle Leslie had a good trick with a cigarette, but Prosser had an even better one with the sun. Here we go now, look over there past my shoulder, across the black wing, watch it rise, watch it rise. And now, down we go, down another 10,000 feet and wait for it, watch, the sun comes up once more. The ordinary miracle occurs. Do it again? No, not unless you want to join the submarine boys.

'You try.' Relaxing had made things easier for Dr Headley's demonstration; the only trouble was, Jean hadn't listened to a word of it. Now, as she tentatively grasped the slippery cap, compressed it into a figure of eight, and began to feed it into herself with no clear sense of direction, she concentrated and tensed. Dr Headley, squatting on a stool and holding her wrist, was trying to guide her. Let's get it over with, Jean thought at one point, and pushed hard. Ouch. *Ouch*.

'No, no, silly girl. Now look what you've done. It's all right, just a bit of healthy blood.' Dr Headley was busy with a towel and some warm water. Then after a while she said, 'Shall we go on?'

Jean slipped back to a bright, cloudless dawn over the Channel and listened to Dr Headley as if over the R/T. This side up, figure of eight, neck of the womb, rim fitting neatly, comfortable, then later, hook the finger, pull. Instructions for some aerial manoeuvre. This made it all seem less humiliating; and less to do with her.

'You may bleed just a little more,' said Dr Headley.

Then Jean was given final instructions on using the cap. When to put it in; how long afterwards to take it out; how to wash it, dry it, powder it, and put it away in its tin until next time. This reminded her of Father and his pipe: he always seemed to spend much longer filling and cleaning and poking it than he ever did smoking it. But perhaps all pleasures were like that.

On the blacked-out train from Paddington, she found herself wondering if she had, as she supposed, lost her virginity. Had she? She felt as if she had — or rather, she felt as she imagined she would if she had done so in the normal way. She felt burst; she felt interfered with. *The rift in the lute* — she didn't know what that meant, but it sounded right. In her handbag was a small cardboard box; she didn't know what to think about it. Was it a protector or an aggressor? Was it a protector that helped aggressors like Michael? Had she lost her virginity to it — or to a cousin from the same batch at the factory? Was she being silly and melodramatic? It was all for Michael, anyway. Worse things could happen. Worse things were happening and most of them to men. You had to do your bit, didn't you?

The box in her handbag intimidated her; it made the ticket collector at the station loom like a customs officer. Any contraband with you, missie? No, nothing to declare. One explosive device. One rifted lute. One slightly bloodstained nether garment.

Dr Headley and the box had made everything seem certain and immutable. But this certainty didn't bring confidence. She didn't find herself looking forward to being in bed with Michael. Of course she loved him, of course it would be all right; of course he would know everything, and instinct would make up for any mutual ignorances. It would be beautiful; it might even be spiritual, as some people said; but what a pity some parts of it had to be so matter-of-fact. And would this matter-of-factness interfere with her responses? Would the Box affect her Periodicity of Recurrence?

When Jean got home, she surprised herself by turning again to Mrs Barrett's little maroon book. She turned to the chapter called The Fundamental Pulse, serious now to find out what the promised deed would be like. Some people, she read, thought of it as a simple wave-pattern of crests and hollows; but it was more complicated than that. 'We have all,' the author of *Our Ostriches* explained,

> at some time, watched the regular ripples of the sea breaking against a sand-bank, and noticed that the influx of another current of water may send a second system of waves at right-angles to the first, cutting athwart them, so that the two series of waves pass through each other.

Jean hadn't ever been to the seaside, but she tried to imagine the pattern of cross-ripples. She heard gulls squawk, and saw untrodden sand. It all sounded quite pleasant. Quite pleasant, but not very important. Maybe it *was* just funny?

Uncle Leslie wasn't at the wedding. Uncle Leslie had done a bunk. Jean's parents were there, and Michael's tall, long-nosed mother who was either awkward or patronizing, Jean couldn't decide, and a policeman friend of Michael's who was best man and who whispered to her beforehand, 'If I'm the best man why are you marrying the other fellow?' (which Jean didn't think was an appropriate remark), and a cousin of Michael's from Wales who had come down specially; but Uncle Leslie wasn't there. One small family marrying into another small family: seven people who didn't know each other very well trying to judge the right degree of celebration for a mufti wedding in wartime. Uncle Leslie would have ignored the niceties and insisted on a knees-up; he might have made a speech or done some tricks. Perhaps she missed him more because as a child she had planned to marry him. His absence seemed a double desertion. But then, Uncle Leslie had done a bunk.

This, at any rate, had been her father's interpretation of events. Uncle Leslie, having lived in England all his life, had caught a boat to New York shortly after Chamberlain's return from Munich. Leslie's summary of the facts, in a much debated letter from Baltimore, ran as follows: Chamberlain had proclaimed peace in our time, Leslie realized he wasn't getting any younger and had decided to see the world, not long after he got to America the war had quite unexpectedly broken out, he was (just) too old to serve in uniform, there wasn't any point in bringing another mouth to feed all the way across the Atlantic, the best thing to do was send food parcels as soon as he'd got set up in a job, and of course he'd join the American Army if the Yanks got involved in the kerfuffle, always assuming they'd have him, and by the way, he thought he'd left a blazer at his last digs, and it would be a shame if it got the moth.

Father's summary of the facts to Mother was rather different: I always knew your brother was a bit of a spiv, too old for the army stuff and nonsense what's wrong with the Home Guard or firewatching or working in a munitions factory, not that your brother ever liked getting his hands dirty or using a spot of elbow grease, just because he sends food parcels he thinks that makes it all right, what's for dinner tonight Mother a little bit of Conscience Pie followed by a slice of Conscience Pudding, well we may as well eat the stuff it'll only go bad, but what does he mean by sending our Jean fancy underwear she's only just had her plait cut off, I won't see my daughter wearing things like this when the bombers are coming over it's not decent, if he joins the American Army I'll swim the North Sea, perhaps our Hero of the Stratosphere on my right would like another slice of Conscience Pudding, it may taste sour but there's no point in letting it go to waste.

In the first two years of the war they ate a lot of Conscience Pie. Father confiscated the underwear but handed it over to Jean when she married. This was Uncle Leslie's only wedding present; she had written to give him the news, but he didn't reply. Uncle Leslie went silent for the rest of the war. Father's speculations on the reason were not always well received by Mother.

When she married, Jean knew the following things:

how to make beds with hospital corners;
how to sew, patch and knit;
how to make three sorts of pudding;
how to lay a fire and blacken a grate;
how to make old pennies bright again by soaking them in
   vinegar;
how to iron a man's shirt;
how to plait hair;
how to insert a Dutch cap;
how to bottle fruit and make jam;
how to smile when she didn't feel like smiling.

She was proud of these accomplishments, though she did not consider them an entirely adequate dowry. She wished, for instance, that she knew the following:

how to dance the waltz, quickstep and polka, for which there
   had been little call so far in her life;
how to run without automatically folding her arms across her
   chest;
how to know in advance whether her remarks were stupid or
   intelligent;
how to predict the weather from a hanging piece of seaweed;
how to tell why a chicken had stopped laying;
how to judge when people were making fun of her;
how to be helped into a coat without getting embarrassed;
how to ask the right questions.

Michael fiddled some petrol and they spent their honeymoon at a pub in the New Forest which had a few rooms above the bar. They drove down late on the Saturday afternoon. As they neared Basingstoke it began to get dark, and they proceeded on side-lights because of the blackout. Jean wondered how good Michael's night vision was; he hadn't been trained like Prosser. She felt frightened: in the first months of the war, she remembered, more people had been killed on the roads than by the enemy. She laid a hand on Michael's arm at one point; but he seemed to misinterpret this, and went faster.

When they were shown to their room, Jean was daunted by the size of the bed. It looked enormous, threatening, active. It was telling her things, mocking and scaring her at the same time. Sporadic murmurs rose through the floor from the bar beneath. She turned her head into Michael's shoulder and said,

'Can we be friends tonight?'

There was a pause, and a slight stiffening of his hand on her neck. Then he said,

'Of course. It's been a long drive.' He stroked her hair a little, then went off for a wash. Over dinner he was jovial and relaxed; he had telephoned his mother and asked her to pass on news of their arrival to the Serjeants. Jean rather wished she could have talked to her mother — a final briefing before the op — but what Michael had done was obviously for the best. She loved him very much, told him so, and asked if she could get into bed and turn out the light while he was in the bathroom. She lay between the sheets with a laundry smell in her nose and wondered what lay ahead. Outside it was a cloudless night and a full summer moon hung in the sky like a pathfinder's flare; a bombers' moon, they called it.

The next day they went for a walk in the morning, because it wasn't right to waste petrol even on their honeymoon, came back to the pub for lunch, walked again in the afternoon, washed and changed; and as they were going down for dinner, Jean asked,

'Can we be friends tonight?'

'I'll have to rape you if this goes on,' he replied with a smile.

'That's what I'm afraid of.'

'Well, you'll have to let me kiss you tonight. No rolling over.'

'All right.'

'And with the lights on.'

The third evening, Jean said, 'Perhaps tomorrow.'

'*Perhaps*? For Christ's sake, we're half-way through our bloody honeymoon. We might as well have gone hiking or something.' His face seemed very red as he stared at her. She felt frightened: not just because he was angry, but because she realized he could get angrier. She also thought: hiking, that sounds nice.

'All right, tomorrow.'

But the next night she developed a stomach cramp shortly after dinner, and the matter had to be postponed. She could sense Michael getting crosser. She had heard, somewhere, that men needed physical release more than women. What happened if they were denied it? Did they blow up, like a car radiator? On the fifth evening, they talked less over dinner. Michael ordered a brandy. Suddenly, Jean whispered,

'Come up in twenty minutes.'

She collected the Box and went to the bathroom along the passage. She lay on the floor with her heels on the edge of the bath and tried to insert her cap. Something was wrong with her muscles. She wondered, briefly, if she should turn out the light and think of Prosser in his black Hurricane with a red glow on his face and hands; perhaps that would relax her. But she knew it was wrong. Instead, she tried squatting; but after some initial success the cap shot out of her and messed the bathmat. She tried again with her legs up; now it was beginning to hurt. She washed the black rubber monster, dried and powdered it, then put it back in its tin.

She lay in bed and listened to the rumble of voices in the bar below. Michael seemed to be taking a long time. Perhaps he was having another brandy. Perhaps he had run off with someone who wasn't defective.

He didn't bother with the bathroom, just stood in the dark discarding his clothes; she tried to guess from the noises which items were being unbuttoned and pulled off. She heard a drawer squeak, and imagined him putting on his pyjamas. There was a whoop of conversation from the bar below. He climbed into bed, kissed her on the cheek, rolled on top of her, pulled up her winceyette nightdress and tugged at the pyjama cord he'd only just tied. *Sex-hyphen*, she suddenly remembered.

The lubricating jelly had given her a surrogate wetness, which seemed to flatter him. After some hunting around, he pushed into her with less difficulty than either of them had imagined. Even so, it hurt. She lay there, waiting for him to say something. When, instead, he began to move up and down inside her, she murmured, very politely, 'I'm afraid I couldn't get my thing in, darling.'

'Oh,' he said, in a curious, neutral voice, a voice from his job. 'Oh.' He didn't sound cross or disappointed, as she had expected him to. Instead, he began pushing harder into her, and just as she was starting to panic at the assault, he gave a high nasal wheeze, pulled out, and ejaculated on her stomach. It was all very unexpected. It was like someone being sick over you, she thought.

When he half-rolled away, she said, 'I'm soaked. You've soaked me.'

'It always feels as if there's more than there really is,' he replied. 'It's like blood.'

They were both silent at that sentence, at its implications as well as its mention of blood. He was panting slightly. She could smell brandy. She lay there with the bar talk rumbling on below as if nothing at all had happened anywhere in the world; she lay there in the dark, thinking about blood. Black and red, black and red, the colours of Prosser's universe. Perhaps they were the only colours in the world when you came down to it.

'I'll get you a handkerchief,' Michael said eventually.

'Don't put the light on.'

'No.'

Another drawer squeaked, and he passed her a handkerchief. It felt the size of a headscarf. She laid it over her stomach, put her hand on it, and rubbed gently in a circular motion. The gesture children use to indicate hunger. Except that someone had just been sick over her. She screwed the handkerchief into a ball, threw it out of bed, pulled down her nightdress, and rolled over on her side.

The next morning she kept her eyes closed when she heard

Michael wake. He came back whistling from the bathroom, dressed, gave her a shake, slapped her chummily on the hip, and murmured, 'See you down there, darling.'

Perhaps it was all right. She dressed quickly and hurried down. Yes, it did seem to be all right, or so she judged from the way he kept passing her too much toast and topping up her cup before it was empty. Perhaps he didn't think she was defective; perhaps he wouldn't send her back.

She had to say something about it, though. This was what happened in marriage, after all. That evening, as they changed for dinner, she found courage when his back was turned. 'I'm sorry about last night.'

He didn't answer. He probably was cross. She started again. 'I'm sure . . . I'm sure next time . . . '

He came round to where she was sitting on the bed and sat half beside her, half behind her. He put a big finger to her lips. 'Shh,' he went. 'It's quite all right. It's natural you're highly strung at this sort of time. I won't make a nuisance of myself again before we leave.'

That wasn't what she wanted to hear at all. It was kind enough, but it seemed almost to be changing the subject. She had to try again. They weren't like their parents, after all, were they: they had read books, and Michael, presumably, had been to the brothels in London. She took his finger from her lips.

'I'll manage next time,' she said, beginning to shake a little; though perhaps this was because Michael was gripping her shoulder rather hard.

'We aren't talking about it,' he said firmly. 'That's enough now. You'll do.' He placed both hands over her face in a soap-smelling caress. One covered the top of her face down to the tip of her nose; the other covered her mouth and chin. A little light peeped in between two of his slightly parted fingers. He held her there for a while, in the soft cage of his hands.

For the last two nights of their honeymoon he didn't trouble her. They returned to live in the two rooms Michael's gaunt mother had allotted them in her square, cold house. The first week was not a success. Either she had a sticky-fingered struggle with her diaphragm, only to find that Michael stayed up late talking to his mother; or she didn't bother, and found him pressing up hard against her. She would go off to the bathroom, struggle and panic, then return and find him asleep, or feigning sleep.

'Michael,' she said, the second time this happened. He grunted. 'Michael, what is it?'

'Nothing,' he said, in a voice that meant: Something.

'Tell me.' No reply. 'Go on.' No reply. 'I can't be expected to guess.'

Eventually, in a weary voice, he replied, 'It's meant to be spontaneous.'

'Oh dear.'

The following night, with help from a little drink, Michael elaborated. It's no good if it isn't spontaneous; and for want of better, or any other, information, she agreed. It's awful if everything's cut and dried. There's something sickening about getting on the boil, pardon the expression, and then having to go off the boil for ten minutes or so; she agreed, blushing inwardly and wondering how long other women took. They couldn't go on having this charade, never coinciding, like the weathermen on a cuckoo clock; she agreed. It would probably help matters — just to begin with, just until they knew one another better — if they decided on certain days when she would . . . put her thing in; not, of course, that this necessarily . . .; she agreed. It seemed to him, thinking it over, that Saturday was one obvious time, because there was always Sunday morning as well if he was too tired on Saturday night; and perhaps Wednesday as well, at least as long as his current shift pattern continued. She agreed, she agreed. Saturday and Wednesday, she said to herself, on Saturday and Wednesday we shall be spontaneous.

The system worked quite well. She got better at handling the Box; Michael didn't hurt her; she became used to the noises he made — the sort of noises you normally associated with small mammals. There was something distinctly nice about sex, she decided, about having your husband's sex-hyphen joined to you, about feeling him turn childish in your arms.

Even so, it did leave her with quite a lot of time for thought. This wasn't, after all, the time when she most loved Michael; she wished it were, but it wasn't. As for the feelings she had in what Dr Headley would have referred to as her nether regions ... well, where were all these interlocking cross-currents she had been led to expect? Where was the honk of gulls and that pure stretch of sand now bearing a single trail of footprints — footprints whose toes pointed outwards? It wasn't like anything she'd ever experienced before. Or was it? Slowly, a memory clarified itself. Yes, that was it: down at the Old Green Heaven with Uncle Leslie, playing the Shoelace Game. That's what it was like: ticklish, and nice, and a bit funny, and different.

She began to laugh as she remembered, but this disturbed Michael, and she turned the laugh into a cough. What a coincidence. But then she'd always known that sex was funny. It was what she had told Dr Headley. Silly Dr Headley.

And that was it, she supposed, lying there one night beneath Michael. That was her life. She didn't feel self-pity about this, merely recognized it. You were born, you grew up, you got married. People pretended — perhaps they really believed — that when you got married it was the start of your life. But it wasn't like that. Getting married was an end, not a beginning: why else did so many films and books finish at the altar? Getting married was an answer, not a question. This wasn't a matter for complaint, simply a matter for observation. You got married, and that was you settled.

Settled. They used that word a lot. Settling down; getting settled; settle yourself. What else did you settle, Jean wondered. Of course, a bill. You owed money, and you settled the bill. It was like that with growing up. Your parents looked after you, and they expected something from you in return, even if neither of you defined that expectation. There was some bill to be paid. Marriage settled the account.

It didn't mean you would be happy ever after. It didn't mean

62

that. It just meant you were settled. You'll do: Michael had said that, just as Mother had. You'll do. Some test had been passed. Even if you were unhappy, you would be looked after. That was what happened, that was what she had seen. There would be children, of course, and this always made the man more responsible. Not that Michael wasn't responsible: he was a policeman, after all. And she would spruce him up a little. There would be a house. There would be children. The war would end. She was a big girl now. She was still — she still could be — Michael's little girl; but that was another matter. She was grown-up. The children would confirm that. Their helplessness would prove that she was grown-up, that she was settled.

The next morning, alone, she looked in the mirror. Brown hair which had lost its childhood yellow. Blue eyes with flecks of indeterminate colour in them, like knitting wool. A squarish jaw which no longer dissatisfied her. She tried smiling at herself, but it didn't really work. She would do, she supposed; she wasn't pretty, and she wasn't complacent, but she would do.

As she stared into the mirror and the knitting-wool eyes stared back, Jean felt that now she knew all the secrets; all the secrets of life. There was a dark, warm cupboard; she had taken out something heavy, wrapped in brown paper. There was no need to cheat — no need to unscrew a tiny viewing-hole and peer in with a torch. She was grown-up. She could carefully and seriously unwrap the paper. She knew what she would find. Four slim ochre points. Golf tees. Of course. What else would you expect? Only a child would take them for hyacinths. Only a child would expect them to sprout. Grown-ups knew that golf tees never sprouted.

TWO

Three wise men — are you serious?

graffito, c.1984

Michael struck fire with his heels. That was how, in later years, Jean was to remember him. In the toolshed he kept a shoemaker's last — a heavy, three-footed iron object, like the coat of arms from some comic country — and on it he would hammer steel corners into the heels of each new pair of shoes he bought. Then he would walk ahead of her, a little too quickly, so that every few strides she would have to break into a clumsy half-run. And as he walked she would hear the sliding scrape of a carving knife on a back step, and fire would be struck from the pavement.

Jean's marriage lasted twenty years. After the guilty disappointment of the honeymoon came the longer, slower dismay of living together. Perhaps she had imagined too strongly that it would be just like not living together: that the life of high, airy skies and light, loose clouds would continue — a life of goodnight kisses, excited greetings, silly games and unspoken hopes miraculously fulfilled. Now she found the hopes had to be spoken if they were to come to anything, and the games seemed far too silly if played by only one person; as for the excited greetings, they followed so closely upon the goodnight kisses, and so regularly, that they could hardly stay excited all the time. No doubt it was the same for Michael, too.

But what puzzled her was how closely you could live beside someone without any sense of intimacy — or what she had always imagined intimacy to be. They lived, ate, slept together, they had jokes no one else could decipher, they were familiar with one another down to their underclothes; but what seemed to emerge from all this were mere patterns of behaviour rather than prized familiarities of response. Jean had imagined — hadn't she? — that the honeysuckle would wrap itself round the hawthorn, that the saplings planted side by side would twine themselves into an arch, that a pair of spoons would nestle their contours together, that two would become one. Silly, picture-book thinking, she realized. She could still love Michael even if she couldn't read his mind or predict his responses; he could still love her even if he seemed complacent about her inner life. A spoon couldn't nestle with a knife, that was all. It had been a mistake to imagine that marriage could alter mathematics. One plus one always made two.

Men changed when they married you; that was what the village women promised. You wait, my girl, they had said. So Jean was only half-surprised by the slow dulling of enjoyment and the arrival of tired discourtesies. What dismayed her more was how the very kindness and gentleness Michael had displayed while courting her now became a source of irritation to him. It seemed to make him cross that he was expected after marriage to behave as he had done before; and this crossness was itself a source of further crossness. Look, he seemed to say, you think that earlier I was deceiving you about what I was really like, don't you. I wasn't. I wasn't cross then and I am cross now: how dare you accuse me of dishonesty? But it struck Jean as a matter of small importance whether or not he had been honest then, if he was cross now.

Of course, it must be largely her fault. And it was, she supposed, normal that her inability to bear a child should set off inexplicable rages in Michael. They were inexplicable not because there wasn't a cause — or at least a justification — but because her inability to conceive remained constant, yet his rages were always untimely.

At first he had wanted to send her to a specialist. But she remembered the previous occasion when he had persuaded — no, tricked — her into going to London. One Dr Headley was enough specialists for a lifetime. So she refused.

'Perhaps I just need some Alpine air,' she said.

'What *do* you mean?'

'Alpine air restores the vitality of the subject.' She quoted it like a proverb.

'Jean, darling.' He took her wrists and squeezed them as if he were about to say something affectionate. 'Has anyone ever told you how abysmally stupid you are?'

She looked away; he held her wrists; she knew she would have to look at him — or at least reply — before he would let go of her. What was the point of him being nasty to her? She probably was stupid, though she half-suspected she might not be; but even so, why should that make him cross? She hadn't been any more intelligent when he met her, and he'd seemed not to mind it then. She felt a pain in her stomach.

Finally, with a small measure of defiance, but not looking him in the face, she said, 'You promised you wouldn't send me back if I was defective.'

'What?'

'When I went to see Dr Headley, I asked if you'd send me back if I was defective. You said no.'

'What's that got to do with anything?'

'Well, if you do think I'm defective, you can send me back.'

'Jean.' He held her wrists more tightly, but still she declined to look at that big red face on the boyish neck. 'Christ. Look.' He sounded exasperated. 'Look, I love you. Christ. Look, I love you. It's just that I sometimes wish you were . . . different.'

Different. Yes, she could see that was what he wanted. She was abysmally stupid and childless. He wanted her intelligent and pregnant. It was as simple as this. *Heads we have six children, Tails we keep a cat.* They would have to buy a cat.

'I've got a pain,' she said.

'I love you,' he replied, almost shouting with exasperation. For the first time, after five years of marriage, this information failed to move her. She didn't disbelieve him, but the whole thing was way beyond a question of honesty now.

'I've got a pain,' she repeated, feeling cowardly about her

inability to face him. No doubt he despised her additionally for having a pain.

Eventually, he let go of her wrists. But over the following months he returned to the question of her 'seeing a specialist'. Jean agreed to the evasive terminology, though inwardly she rehearsed phrases she had read while Sun-Up Prosser snored in the next room. *Maladjustment of the organs*, she remembered, and *congestion of the womb*. Congestion — she thought of men coming to unblock the drains, and shuddered. Barren, that was the proper word, the biblical word. Barren. And barrenness. Barrenness made her think of the Gobi desert, which made her think of Uncle Leslie. Don't let the club-head drop or there'll be more sand flying than on a windy day in the Gobi desert. She saw a golfer in a bunker, hacking, hacking, hacking with his club and the ball never coming out.

At times, though, she wondered if her condition was quite the failing Michael obviously thought it. During their courtship she had found herself tensing whenever he mentioned children. One thing at a time, she had thought. And then her experience of the first thing had made her a little sceptical about the second.

Perhaps she was unnatural, rather than barren. Or as well as being barren. Abysmally stupid, barren and unnatural: that was how she must look from the outside. It felt different from the inside. She could shrug off being barren and unnatural, if that was how people found her. As for being abysmally stupid, she could see Michael's point, but she could also see beyond it. It seemed to Jean that intelligence wasn't as pure and unalterable a characteristic as people believed. Being intelligent was like being good: you could be virtuous in one person's company and yet wicked in another's. You could be intelligent with one person and stupid with another. It was partly to do with confidence. Though Michael was her husband, who had led her from virginity and adolescence to womanhood and maturity (or so the world presumed), who had protected her physically and financially, who had awarded her the name of Curtis in exchange for that of Serjeant, he had strangely failed to give her confidence. In a way she had been more confident when she had been eighteen and foolish. At twenty-three, with Michael, she felt less confident, and therefore less intelligent. It seemed an unkind turn of events: first Michael made her less intelligent, and then he despised her for being what he had made her.

Perhaps he had made her barren too. Was that possible? Anything, she thought, was possible. So the next time they argued about her defectiveness, she looked up, held his eye, and quickly, before the courage went, said,

'I'll go if you go.'

'What do you mean?'

'I'll go if you go.'

'Jean, don't talk like a child. Repeating yourself is not the same as explaining yourself.'

'Perhaps you're the one that's defective.'

That was when he hit her. It was, in fact, the only time in their life together that he did, and it was less a punch than an awkward round-arm cuff which landed where her shoulder joined her neck; but she was not to know at the time. As she ran from the room, words seemed to descend on her from all angles. *Bitch*, she heard the first time, and *imbecile*, and *woman*, this last word beaten and sharpened until it had an edge for slashing with.

The words continued to be thrown after she had shut the door behind her. But its presence emptied them of meaning: two inches of close-fitting wood drained a violent anatomy of your character into mere noise. It felt as if Michael were throwing objects at her which all made the same sound as they hit the door: was that a plate, an inkwell, a book, a knife, or a tomahawk hung with feathers and still sharp despite its many previous victims? She couldn't tell.

She was grateful for this, as she thought back over the incident in the next few days, as she accepted Michael's apologies and declined his caresses. Sticks and stones may break my bones, but words will never hurt me: why did people formulate such proverbs, unless they feared all too accurately that the opposite was the case? Pains healed, she knew (that first wound in her

71

stomach had gone within the hour), but words festered. *Woman*, Michael had shouted at her, screwing the sound up into a ball first so that he could throw it farther and more accurately. *Woman*, where the word itself carried no venom, but the poison was all in the tone. *Woman*, two anodyne syllables which he redefined for her: *all that exasperates me* was the new meaning.

After that, they stopped discussing children. Over the years they continued to make love, perhaps once a month, or at least whenever Michael seemed to want to; but Jean felt passive about the whole business. When she thought of Michael and sex she imagined an over-filling water-tank which occasionally had to be drained; it didn't have to be done too often, it wasn't exactly a nuisance, it was just part of running the house. As for herself and sex, she preferred not to think about it. Sometimes she pretended to more pleasure than she felt; this was only polite. She didn't find sex funny any more; she just found it ordinary. And all those phrases she had once learnt — silly, exciting phrases which had seemed to flirt with her — now came from a very long time ago, from the island of childhood. The island you could not leave without getting wet. She thought of two wave patterns meeting at right-angles, and felt a little guilty. As for those slogans — the one about the curve of normal desire and the other about the feeble and transient up-welling in women suffering from fatigue and overwork — they seemed like faded graffiti briefly glimpsed on the wall of a country bus-shelter.

She didn't need any Alpine air; and the fatigue she suffered from was not physical in origin. She kept house for Michael; she gardened; she owned a succession of pets, aware that the village considered them substitutes for children. She kept a pig that escaped and was found eating the cat's-eyes in the middle of the road. She had dealings with secret animals, the ones who would come only when she was out of the way. At times, lying in bed, she would hear the hedgehog rattling its jampot-lid of milk as if in thanks, and she would smile.

For twenty years she maintained a normal part in village life; she took tea; she helped, she donated; she became, in her own

72

mind, rather anonymous. She wasn't miserable, though she was scarcely happy; she was well enough liked, without joining any of the village's central conspiracies; she was, she slowly decided, rather ordinary. Michael certainly thought her ordinary. But there were worse things than that. As a child, she had sometimes thought she might become special, or at least wife to someone special; but then all children thought that, didn't they? Extra flesh softened the angles of her face. A low, grey sky, in which single clouds could scarcely be discerned, always threatened rain.

At times, over the years, she wondered if Michael might be having an affair. There were no lipsticked collars or furtive photographs, there was no hurried replacing of the telephone; but then, given Michael's profession, there probably wouldn't be. The only evidence came from the way he sometimes looked at her, as if peering down from 18,000 feet towards a smoking merchantman. She never asked; he never volunteered. Who could tell about another life?

Her parents died. When she was thirty-eight her periods stopped, a matter neither for surprise nor regret: her existence, she felt, had long since finished defining itself. Did she sometimes want to scream in the middle of the night? Who didn't? She had only to look at the lives of other women to realize things could be worse. Her first grey hair appeared, and she did nothing about it.

Almost a year after her periods stopped she became pregnant. She made the doctor test her twice before accepting his decision. He said that such things were not unknown, and murmured with a polite vagueness about trains to London. Jean thanked him briskly, and went home to tell Michael.

She wasn't really aware that she was testing him, though in later years admitted to herself that she must have been. At first he was cross, in an unfamiliar way, almost cross with himself; perhaps he wanted to accuse her of having an affair but couldn't, either because of the improbability or his own bad conscience. Then he said firmly that it was too late for them to have children, and that she should get rid of it. Then he remarked on what a strange turn of events it had been after twenty-odd years. Then he elaborated, declaring the whole story pretty rum and chuckling at the surprise the chaps would get. Then a relaxed, bovine expression came into his face, and he went silent; perhaps he was playing out short scenes of paternity in his head. Finally, he turned to Jean and asked what she thought about it all.

'Oh, I'm going to have the baby and leave you.' She had not intended to say anything like this at all; but somehow the words, spoken out of instinct and with no conscious courage, failed to surprise her. They seemed not to surprise Michael either; he just laughed.

'There's mah lass,' he said in a funny accent she would normally have found embarrassing; now, she just found it puzzling. Michael clearly didn't understand anything about anything.

'But I expect I'll leave you and then have the baby. I expect I'll do it that way round.' Again, the words failed to surprise her; now that she was rehearsing them, they seemed not merely irrefutable, but almost a banality. She felt no fear, either, even though she expected Michael to be cross.

Instead, he patted her on the arm, said, 'We'll talk about it in the morning', and started telling her about a series of clothing thefts from a local department store which had finally been cleared up. A two-way mirror had been installed in a ladies' changing-room, and an alarmed detective-sergeant, crouching in a cupboard, had apprehended a transvestite shop-lifter stuffing blouses into his bra.

She wanted to say, Look, it's not really anything to do with you; the decision, that is. I want a more difficult life, that's all. What I really want is a first-rate life. I may not get it, but the only chance I have lies in getting out of a second-rate life. I may fail completely, but I do want to try. It's to do with me, not you; so don't worry.

But she wouldn't be able to say any of this. There was a decorum to be observed, like the decorum about whether or not Michael had affairs. You had to obey certain rules, permit certain

74

angers, respect certain forms of lying; you had to appeal to feelings in the other person which both of you pretended were there even if you suspected they weren't. This, of course, was part of what she meant by a second-rate life.

She realized that Michael might be hurt by her departure; but this awareness, instead of urging her to stay, made her slightly despise him. She felt no pride at such a reaction, but couldn't deny it. For the first time in their marriage she knowingly had a certain power over him. Perhaps power always encouraged contempt — perhaps this was why he had thought her abysmally stupid. If so, there was all the more reason for leaving.

She wanted to go at once, but didn't. It was best for the child, she decided, if it slept through its first months without too many dinning reverberations from the life ahead, the life outside; better not to start its troubles before she had to. And there was a little farewell consideration to be had for Michael. If she vanished now, a couple of months pregnant, the village would mutter that she had run away to join a lover, some tea-dance gigolo or circus strongman. Whereas if she left with the child, or in late pregnancy, they wouldn't know what to believe. Perhaps they'd think she had gone mad. Women often went mad, it was said, after giving birth; no doubt the probability was greater in a woman of her age.

Neighbours told her that a late child was a blessed child. The doctor warned her quietly about mongolism, and mentioned trains to London again. Michael watched her warily, moving between boyish self-congratulation and unfocused fear. She sensed this fear, and did nothing to allay it; instead, she used it. She knew that pregnant women were meant to turn in on themselves, that mother and unborn child set up an autonomous republic, and that the old magic of the tribe taught men to behave differently as their wives swelled — taught them an awe which frequently expressed itself in soppiness.

So Jean allowed herself to appear more inward than she really felt. She began to behave capriciously as well, since this was half-expected of her. Sometimes, indeed, she did feel capricious

— the rich, mealy smell as she mixed the chicken feed made her want to put the bucket to her lips and take a swig; but she didn't mention these normal oddities of her condition. Instead, on long afternoon walks beneath a dull grey sky, she practised a wider capriciousness. Deliberately, she behaved against her character and against her feelings. She found herself able to express anger and boredom with Michael, although she never displayed these emotions when she really felt them; she merely tried them out when they might have been appropriate.

Pregnancy seemed to nudge her into wider expectations, and her easy capriciousness whispered like a secret breeze that character need not be fixed. She did not particularly enjoy this phase of dishonesty, but thought it important; she was not yet brave enough to be completely honest. Perhaps that would come with her new life, her second life. She remembered Uncle Leslie's disappointing hyacinths. Well, maybe a tee could sprout. After all, it was made of wood.

*   *   *   *

Under the flat, uncommitted sky of that autumn, with a soft wind parting her mackintosh and showing off her belly, she would sometimes think of Sergeant-Pilot Prosser. His posting had come through a few weeks before the wedding. He had stood by the creosoted gate with the sunrise motif, shifting from one foot to the other, occasionally jerking his head down to check that his case was safely underneath his arm; finally, he smiled without looking at her, and stamped off. Jean had wanted to ask him to the wedding, but Michael had frowned. What had become of Prosser? Jean looked up at the sky, half-expecting it to answer.

Prosser had been brave. He said he was windy, he said he was burnt, but that wasn't the point. There was no courage without fear, and without admitting fear. Men's courage was different from women's courage. Men's courage lay in going out and nearly getting killed. Women's courage — or so everyone said —

lay in endurance. Men showed courage in violent bouts, women in patient stretches. This fitted their natures: men were more prickly, more bad-tempered than women. Perhaps you had to be cross to be brave. Men went out into the world and were brave; women stayed at home and showed courage by enduring their absence. Then, Jean thought wryly, the men came home and were bad-tempered, and the women showed courage by enduring their presence.

She was seven months pregnant when she left Michael; and that morning she shopped for him. There would be difficulties, no doubt, with things like ... well, income tax; but whereas earlier the fretful half-awareness of difficulties might have prevented her departure for years, now such things seemed unimportant. She didn't feel wiser in pregnancy, just that her angle of vision had changed; though this in itself might be a form of wisdom. She thought of other marriages in the village and was relieved hers hadn't been worse. Mrs Lester, who sometimes didn't leave the house for days if the bruising was bad, had once said to her, 'I know he's a bit difficult to control, but who'd do his washing if I left?' To Mrs Lester, the logic had a melancholy perfection; and at the time Jean had nodded agreement and thought that Mrs Lester was a bit simple, though not that simple.

The village women (and Jean did not exclude herself from their number) managed their husbands. They fed them, waited on them, cleaned and washed for them, deferred to them; they accepted men's interpretation of the world. In return, they got money, a roof, security, children and irreversible promotion in the hierarchy of the village. This seemed a good enough deal; and having got it, they patronized their husbands behind their backs, calling them children, talking of their little ways. The husbands, for their part, thought they managed their wives: you had to be firm but fair, they said, but if you let them know who was boss, gave them the housekeeping regular and didn't let on how much you were keeping back for beer money, then things would work out all right.

The partner who left was always the guilty one. 'She just

upped and offed'; 'he walked right out on her'. To leave was to betray; to leave was to give up your rights; to leave showed weakness of character. Stick it out; rough with the smooth; devil you know; ups and downs; can't last for ever. How often had she heard such phrases, cheerfully delivered and cheerfully believed? Running away, people said, showed a lack of courage. Jean wondered if the opposite might be the case.

Abysmally stupid, Michael had said. If I'm abysmally stupid, you can't have been too bright to marry me. That's what she should have replied. Or rather, yes I am abysmally stupid to have put up with you for so long. Except that it hadn't been as bad as all that — Mrs Lester had had it a lot worse. But when Michael had yelled *woman* at her, and the word had screamed its shrapnel round the room, she should have quietly replied, *man*. Meaning: of course you're behaving like this, it must be hard for you too, I pity you. Men should be pitied, Jean thought; pitied, and left. Women were brought up to believe that men were the answer. They weren't. They weren't even one of the questions.

I said I would. That was all she put in the note. She had to leave one, otherwise Michael might get the wrong idea and start dragging the gravel ponds. But she didn't have to give explanations; and above all, she mustn't apologise. *I said I would.* The words, on a blue-lined sheet of writing-paper left on the kitchen table, were weighted down with her two rings: silver with a single garnet for engagement (from Michael's mother), platinum for wedding. As the train took her away, she repeated to herself, *I said I would.* For too long she had listened to, acquiesced in, and herself pronounced a *we* she didn't believe. Now it was *I*. Though soon enough, she supposed, it would be another *we*; but a different one. Mother and child: what sort of a *we* was that? She dug in her handbag and found a thin strip of tin. JEAN SERJEANT XXX, it said reassuringly.

She was unconscious during Gregory's birth. It was better that way, they said; woman of your age, possible complications. She didn't object. When she came round they told her she had a beautiful boy. 'Is he . . . ' — she seemed to be reaching into that

78

part of her brain which was still asleep — 'Is he . . . defective?'
'Perish the thought, Mrs Serjeant,' came the reply, and the tone
was scolding, as if less than perfect children reflected on the
hospital. 'Shame on you. He's got all his working parts.'

He looked much like other babies, and Jean, much like other
mothers, found him perfect beyond the description of poets. He
was an ordinary miracle: a mixture of vulnerability and achievement which kept her oscillating between fear and pride. When
that heavy head flopped backwards on its inadequate cabbage-
stem of neck she prickled with alarm; when the tiny fingers held
her thumb like an athlete gripping wall-bars she felt swathed in
pleasure. At first she seemed to be clearing up after him a lot:
every hole in his body competed to exude the most secretions;
only his ears knew reasonable behaviour. But quickly she got
used to this, and to all the other new smells a baby brought. She
was starting again, that was the important thing to remember;
Gregory had given her the chance to start again. For that, she
would love him even more.

She learned the noises that calmed him, some borrowed from
the days when she kept animals. She clucked and chattered;
sometimes, for a change, she would utter a buzzing noise, as of
an insect, or a distant aeroplane. His first tooth arrived, and she
considered it a world event, something of much greater signi-
ficance than the first Sputnik.

Until he went to school, she took him everywhere with her.
She worked in pubs, cheap restaurants and hamburger bars. She
remembered the reek of fried onions on his nappy; she remembered tucking him away in a back room at the Duke of Clarence
like a secret two-year-old drinker; she remembered his patient,
alert gaze as it took in a sweating cook, a harassed waiter, a
cursing drayman. Her employers often pressed titbits on her to
feed the little fellow up. She clothed him with erratic help from
Uncle Leslie, who had returned from America to Luton, and
who now sent clothes parcels instead of food hampers. Some of
the clothing needed a little alteration. When Gregory was
five, he received for his birthday a double-breasted evening suit,

chest-size 42, a goose-pimple evening shirt and a purple cummerbund.

Gregory complained little. He grew into a quiet, passive boy, his curiosity restrained by fear; he preferred to watch other children play rather than participate himself. They lived in a succession of market towns — the sort of places with a bus garage but no cathedral; Jean was distrustful of village life, and wary of cities. They rented accommodation; they kept to themselves; she tried to forget Michael. Gregory never complained about their peripatetic existence; and when he asked what his father was like, he received answers which were fairly accurate, and which made allusion to stern masters at schools he had already left.

At first they moved house a lot. She rarely passed a policeman without thinking of Michael, and she nervously assumed that the entire force was passing back messages to him. When a constable in the street ducked his head towards his lapel and started confiding in his walkie-talkie, Jean saw Michael sitting in some underground HQ like Winston Churchill. She imagined her face displayed on posters lit by a dim blue lamp. Michael knew exactly where she was and would have them brought back. He would have them brought back in an open wagon. Placards would be hung round their necks, and all the villages would turn out to hiss the fugitive wife. Jean wryly recalled the line of advice from her marriage handbook: *be always escaping.*

Or he would have Gregory taken away from her; that was her more real fear. He would say she had run away and was unfit to bring up her son; that's right, he'd finally get her pronounced defective. He'd say she was irresponsible, he'd say she had affairs. Gregory would be taken away, he would go to live with Michael, Michael would install a mistress and pretend she was a housekeeper. The village would praise him for rescuing his son from a life of vagabondage and prostitution. They would say she had gypsy blood.

So they had to keep on running away. They had to keep on running away, and Jean wasn't to have affairs. Not that she wanted them; and perhaps she was a little frightened of them —

what had Prosser said about getting burned twice? Certainly she was afraid that, if she had them, Gregory would be taken away. There were cases like that in the papers. And so when men approached her, or seemed likely to approach her, and especially when she half-wanted them to, she would become quietly unavailable; she would play with the brass wedding-ring she had bought at a market stall; and she would call Gregory to her. She became a little careless about her appearance; she let her hair streak increasingly with grey; part of her looked forward to the time when she wouldn't have to worry about all that.

Michael didn't pursue her. Many years later she discovered that he used to telephone Uncle Leslie every so often, make him promise silence, and ask for news. Where they were living, how Gregory was doing at school. He never asked them to come back. He didn't install a mistress, or even a housekeeper. He died of a heart attack at fifty-five, and Jean, as she claimed the estate, regarded it as retrospective maintenance.

One Christmas, when he was ten, Gregory received a model aeroplane kit from Uncle Leslie. After the war, Leslie had returned to England with tales — if you would but listen — of extravagant and perilous endeavours: yarns which began with him tapping the side of his nose to indicate that the matter he was about to describe was still hush-hush. But nowadays Jean found she had had enough of masculine adventures. Or perhaps she had grown out of Uncle Leslie: it was a pitiless rule, but you could not remain the same kind of uncle for ever. She was fond of Leslie, but there was no point in children's games between them any more; increasingly, she found herself saying, 'Oh, Leslie, do shut up,' when he was telling Gregory how back in '43 he had piloted a midget sub across the Channel, garrotted a German guard on the beach near Dieppe, scaled a cliff, dynamited the local heavy-water plant, abseiled down again and away. As Leslie would be describing the starless night, and the ripples on the surface as the pocket sub slipped beneath the dark waters, Jean would murmur, 'Oh, Leslie, do shut up' — though she felt unfair when she looked at two disappointed faces. Why was she depriving Gregory of what she had herself enjoyed with Uncle Leslie? Because it wasn't true, she supposed. Leslie was now about seventy, though he would only admit to not seeing twenty-five again. He no longer popped down the Old Green Heaven, except to wash behind his ears. Perhaps all the washing had affected his sense of truth.

The model aeroplane kit was a Lysander, and Gregory worked on it for several days before discovering that the undercarriage and part of the tailplane were missing. Perhaps the model had come from one of Leslie's elaborate bartering arrangements: he seemed to consider money a very primitive form of exchange. Jean went to a model shop and asked about replacement parts; but that particular line had been discontinued some years before.

As consolation, she bought Gregory a Hurricane kit, and proudly half-watched as he cut the first balsa-wood struts. He worked in silence, the light occasionally catching the small brass knife with the curving blade. She liked the aeroplane best when it stood on the wad of newspaper in skeleton form, elegant and unthreatening. Afterwards, it was clothed, and took on hinting seriousness. There was Perspex for the hood, tissue-paper for the wings and fuselage, a yellow plastic propeller and yellow plastic wheels. For a day there was a smell of pear-drops as Gregory applied dope to the aeroplane's skin; the cladding sagged and drooped, then pulled tight as it dried. The instructions suggested painting the Hurricane in camouflage colours: swirling green and brown on its top surfaces, so that it would merge with the English countryside, blue-grey underneath, so that it would merge with the uncertain English sky. Gregory painted it scarlet, all over. Jean was relieved. That lissom outline, familiar from years ago, had pleased but also upset her; now, with its joke colouring and silly yellow wheels, it had ended up as no more than a child's toy.

'When shall we fly it?'

But Gregory shook his head. He was a studious, round-faced ten-year-old, who had just been prescribed glasses. He had built the Hurricane to look at not to fly. If he flew it, it might crash. If it crashed, that would prove he hadn't built it properly. This wasn't worth the risk.

Gregory made a scarlet Hurricane, a purple Spitfire, an orange Messerschmidt and an emerald Zero; he flew none of them. Perhaps he sensed his mother's quiet surprise, and perhaps he understood it as disappointment, because one evening he announced that he had bought a Vampire, that it came with a jet engine, and that he would fly this one. Jean watched yet again the frowning concentration, the tender precision as the glittering knife cut across the grain of the balsa wood. She watched the glue hardening on Gregory's fingertips into a second skin, which he would peel off at the end of the day. She smelt pear-drops, and observed again the cunning way in which a fragile structure acquired strength and taut certainty. The Vampire seemed an awkward aeroplane, with its brief, pod-like fuselage and a tail assembly joined to the wings by long struts. Jean thought it resembled a broad bean in scaffolding — until Gregory painted it gold.

They were renting rooms on the outskirts of Towcester, in a house with a fire-escape zig-zagging down its back wall. Gregory normally distrusted this flaking iron staircase, and feared even those solid platforms where the steps turned; now he showed no apprehension. They stood fifteen feet above the ground; twenty yards away two fir trees marked the end of the garden, and then beyond a ginger beech hedge lay open country-side. The sky was pale autumn blue, with thin, high clouds like vapour-trails; the wind was soft. Perfect flying weather.

Gregory uncapped the small aluminium engine in the Vampire's belly, and inserted a brown cylinder of solid fuel. He pushed an inch of wick through a small hole, held the aeroplane at shoulder-height by its broad-bean fuselage, and asked his mother to light the fuse. When it crackled and flared, Gregory gently launched the Vampire into the welcoming air.

It glided perfectly, as if keen to confirm how meticulous Gregory's craftsmanship had been. The trouble was, it didn't stop gliding: gently, it descended to the lawn beneath, landing without harm. Probably the wick had burnt out too soon and failed to ignite the rocket fuel; or perhaps the fuel was too wet, or too dry, or something. They went down the steps and picked up the shining gold Vampire.

The engine was missing. There was a scorch-mark on the tissue-paper and a hole in the fuselage belly. Jean could see Gregory scowling: the engine must have dropped out during the launch. They searched first at the foot of the staircase, found nothing, and continued down the rough lawn to the point at which the aeroplane had landed. Then they searched at different angles to the flight-path, until the implications of where they were looking amounted to a libel on Gregory's constructional skills; he went silent, and retired to the house. Late in the afternoon, under a disapproving sky, Jean discovered the small aluminium cylinder in the ginger beech hedge beyond the fir trees. There had been nothing wrong with the engine. The engine had certainly flown. It had just left the Vampire behind, that was all.

Gregory gave up making aeroplanes. Soon afterwards, it seemed to Jean, he began to shave; he stopped wearing his child's spectacles with the elasticated metal ear-pieces, and took to a pair of horn-rims; he began to look through his horn-rims at girls. Not all of the girls looked back.

They continued running away even after Michael's death. During his adolescence Gregory knew a dozen schools. At each one, he quickly joined that safe, anonymous band of boys who avoid being bullied without ever becoming popular. No one could object to him; but no one had any particular reason for liking him. From the corner of a dozen playgrounds he watched the noisy fury of others. Jean remembered him at fourteen sitting in a motorway restaurant where she was assistant manageress. The restaurant bridged the road; Gregory was at a table by a murky plate-glass window, playing with a computer chess set Leslie had given him. The machine — which was missing two pawns — would give out little bleeps and pips as it announced its moves and chivvied its opponent. Gregory sat there, smiling benignly at the chequered instrument as if applauding its humanity. Occasionally, when waiting for the computer to make up its mind, he would shift his gaze to the traffic below, to the wailing flow of people quickly going to other places. He stared at them without envy.

Jean didn't. She kept her eyes on her work because it was temptingly easy to look down from that bridge and get tugged away in the slipstream of some family saloon with camping equipment on the top, or some open sports car trailing hair and laughter, or even some filthy van trundling junk from one county to another. How could Gregory sit there so phlegmatically, nodding across at his bleeping friend, untouched by the whirling pull of the traffic? She had a good job at the motorway restaurant, but she did not keep it long.

Finally, when Gregory was old enough to be left, Jean began travelling. There had been some money when her parents died, and more from Michael; Gregory urged her to spend it on herself. Now, in her middle fifties, she felt the desire to be somewhere, anywhere else. She had seen most parts of England while bringing up Gregory; but running away didn't count as travel. A temporary friend explained that her new urge was probably a substitute for sex. 'Spread your wings, Jean,' remarked this girl of twenty-five who had already flapped hers until the membrane was stretched as thin as tissue-paper. Jean thought most things weren't substitutes for other things; they were just themselves. 'I want to travel,' she replied simply.

She didn't want to explore, and wasn't especially adventurous; she just wanted to be somewhere else. At first she took package tours to European cities: three days of blurry coach-rides and dutiful museum visits, three days of asking for things on the menu she hoped would surprise her; mostly they did. She went alone; and if she missed Gregory, she was seldom lonely. She found the simplest things would keep her company: a newspaper whose language she couldn't understand; a dank canal with oil patches full of rainbows; the window display of some primitive

85

chemist or brutal corsetière; street-corner smells of coffee, disinfectant and pigbins.

One autumn Leslie reported a betting coup and bought her a day trip to the Pyramids by Concorde. Such a combination of extravagance and banality: she was too excited to ask her uncle the names of the horses involved. Jean had breakfast high above the browning English wheatfields and a buffet lunch at the Cairo Holiday Inn. She was hustled through the Bazaar; she had a Lawrence of Arabia headdress crammed on her skull for a group photo and was hoisted aboard a camel; finally, she was shown the Pyramids and the Sphinx. How close they were to Cairo: she had always imagined that the Sphinx skulked among the shifting sands, and that the Great Pyramid rose distantly like a mirage from some dangerous moonscape of desert. But it took only a coach-ride through the suburbs of Cairo to discover them. One of the world's Seven Wonders had turned out to be day-tripper material.

Somewhere over the blacked-out Mediterranean, as the aeroplane slipped its lead, a rhyme came into Jean's head, something taught decades earlier by her scripture teacher at the village school:

> The *Pyramids* first, which in Egypt were laid;
> Then *Babylon's Gardens* for Amytis made;
> Third, *Mausolus' Tomb* of affection and guilt . . .

She got stuck. 'Third, *Mausolus' Tomb* of affection and guilt . . .' Guilt, guilt . . . *built*, that was it. 'Of Ephesus built.' What was built at Ephesus — or did it mean by Ephesus? 'Fifth, *Colossus of Rhodes*, cast in brass, to the sun' — the fully formed line suddenly came to her; but she couldn't get much further. Jupiter's something, was it, and something else in Egypt?

Back home, she went to the library and looked up the Seven Wonders of the World, but couldn't find any of the ones from her rhyme. Not the Pyramids even? Or the Hanging Gardens of Babylon? In the encyclopedia it said: the Coliseum of Rome; the Catacombs of Alexandria; the Great Wall of China; Stonehenge;

the Leaning Tower of Pisa; the Porcelain Tower of Nankin; the Mosque of St Sophia of Constantinople.

Well. Perhaps there were two separate lists. Or perhaps they had to update the list every so often as new Wonders got built and old ones fell down. Maybe anyone could make up their own private seven. Why not? She didn't think the catacombs of Alexandria sounded up to much. They might not even be there any more. As for the porcelain tower of Nankin: it sounded extremely improbable that anything made of porcelain could have survived. And if it had, the Red Guards might well have knocked it down.

A plan came into her head to visit these Seven Wonders. She'd already seen Stonehenge; and the Leaning Tower, and the Coliseum, for that matter. If she replaced the Catacombs with the Pyramids, that made four. Which left the Great Wall, the Porcelain Tower and St Sophia. She could do the first two in one trip, and then if the Porcelain Tower didn't exist she'd swap it for Chartres, which she'd already seen. That left St Sophia, but Uncle Leslie had once told her that they ate hedgehogs in Turkey, so she changed it to the Grand Canyon. She was aware that this was cheating a little, as the Canyon wasn't exactly man made, but she gave a little shrug. Who was there to check up on her now?

In June she joined a package tour to China. They went first to Canton, Shanghai and Nanjing (as they now seemed to call it), where she asked the regional guides about the Porcelain Tower. There was a Drum Tower, and a Bell Tower, but nobody had heard of a Porcelain Tower. Just as she had suspected. Her guide book was also silent on the matter: it told her instead that Nanjing was proud of 'Zu Chong zhi, the mathematician who made an approximately correct calculation of *pi*' and 'Fan Zhen, the philosopher famous for his essay, *The Destructibility of the Soul*'. How very strange, Jean thought. Wasn't the soul meant to be some sort of absolute? Either it existed or it didn't exist. How could you destroy one? Perhaps it was just a bad translation. And as for *pi* — wasn't that an absolute as well? What was the point of celebrating an approximately correct calculation, and wasn't this in any case a contradiction in terms? She had expected the Chinese to be a bit different, but this all seemed back to front.

They stayed in Beijing, as Peking now seemed to be called, for three days. On the first they visited the Great Wall, stiffly walking up a short stretch while in the distance the Wall itself airily hurdled the hills. It was the only man-made object visible from the Moon: Jean tried to remember that as she ducked into a dark guard-tower which smelt as rank as a public lavatory. She also noticed the large number of graffiti cut into the top stones of the Wall. Chinese graffiti, so they looked elegant and appropriate. A jovial, red-bearded fellow from the tour, noting Jean's interest, suggested that one of them meant 'Don't shoot until you see the yellows of their eyes.' Jean smiled politely, but her mind was elsewhere. Why did the Chinese cut graffiti into their Wall? Was this a universal instinct, to cut graffiti? Like the universal instinct to try and calculate *pi*, however approximately?

On the second day they visited palaces and museums; on the third, temples and antique shops. At the Temple of Heaven, they were promised, there would be a treat: an echo wall. Jean thought she had once been taken to a whispering gallery — perhaps there was one in the dome of St Paul's — but could no longer tell whether this was a false memory or not.

The Echo Wall was to the south of the main Temple buildings: circular, some thirty or forty yards in diameter, with a single gateway on one side. Groups of Chinese were already trying out the echo as Jean's party arrived. The guide explained that two people could stand at opposite points on the wall's circumference, and by speaking in a normal voice but at a slight angle to the bricks could be heard perfectly by one another. Whether this effect had been planned, or was fortuitous, nobody knew.

Jean walked to the nearest section of the wall. She felt tired now. The air in Beijing was extremely dry, and the fine dust which blew everywhere came straight, they were told, from the Gobi desert. Don't let the club-head drop, Uncle Leslie used to say, or there'll be more sand flying than on a windy day in the Gobi desert. Michael had thought her as barren as the Gobi desert. Dust got in her eyes, and she felt a brisk sadness descend upon her. An echo wall was not something you should visit alone, any more than you should take a solitary ride in the Tunnel of Love. She missed ... somebody, she didn't know who. Not Michael; perhaps some version of Michael, someone still around and still companionable, who might tramp across to the other side of the wall, cough into it in her direction, then wander back to the middle and grumble that the thing didn't work properly and hadn't they ever heard of Indian tea in China? Someone a bit grumpy but who was never serious about being grumpy. Someone who might bore her but would never frighten her.

Small hope. She leaned against the wall and pressed her ear close to the bricked curve. There was some indistinguishable muttering and then, with sudden clarity, a pair of Western voices.

'Go on.'

'No, you first.'

'Go on.'

'I'm shy.'

'*You're* not shy.'

The voices presumably belonged to a couple on Jean's tour, but she couldn't yet identify them. The wall seemed to drain off individuality from the voices, leaving them as all-purpose Western, male and female.

'Do you think this place is bugged?'

'Whatever gives you that idea?'

'I think there's a chap listening in. Do you see, that fellow in the Mao cap?'

Jean looked up. A few yards in front of her an elderly Chinese in an olive jacket and Mao cap was tortoising his head towards the wall. The Western voices were beginning to be recognizable: they belonged to a young couple, brash and rather too recently married for the general comfort of the tour.

'Mao Tse-tung had a big yellow ding-dong.'

'Vincent! For Christ's sake!'

'Just trying it on to see if old Mao-cap understands English.'

'Vincent! Say something else. Say something clean.'

'All right.'

'Go on then.'

'Are you ready?'

'Yes. Go on.'

'You've got great legs.'

'Oh, Vincent, have I?'

Jean left them to it, with the elderly Chinese still craned into their conceited endearments. Which was better: to understand nothing, like him, or everything, like her?

Apart from *pi* and the question of the soul, Jean found China less strange and more comprehensible than she had imagined. True, parts of it were like listening to some gnomic voice come muttering off the great curve of a dusty wall. But more often, it was like hearing your own language spoken confidently and yet with different emphases. 'In Asian times . . .' The tour guides would often start a sentence like this; and at first Jean believed what she heard — that the Chinese referred to the old days as the Asian times, because that was when their civilization had been at its most dominant. Even when she knew they meant *ancient*, Jean preferred to hear *Asian*. In Asian times . . .

'In the fields we grow wheat and lice.' Other members of the tour, especially the brash young couple, giggled; but Jean preferred this alternative language. 'In the fields there are sugar beet, potatoes and ladies.' 'In 1974 the temple was repented.' 'Now here we are at the sobbing centre.' Even Jean smiled at that one, heard in Canton; but she smiled at its aptness. Westerners descended from their buses to spend money on things most Chinese would never be able to afford. Rightly was it called the sobbing centre: Canton's wailing wall.

No, this land wasn't really so strange. There was much poverty and simplicity in the countryside, but it struck Jean in images which might almost have come from her own childhood:

a pig, roped to the pannier of a bicycle, on its way to market; an old woman, buying two eggs from a stall, holding them up to the light in fierce examination; the verbal clatter of bartering; the damp, straddle-legged ritual with the plough; and the patching of clothes. This activity, which since the war had largely died out in the West, was vigorously alive: in a tiny Szechuan village, where the bus stopped for lavatories and photographs, she saw a patched tea-towel hanging up to dry. The washing-line was a bamboo pole slung between the branches of a banyan tree; the tea-towel contained more patching than it did original cloth.

Old poverty looked familiar; and the images of new money were even more familiar: the large radios, the Japanese cameras, the bright clothing which avoided blue and green, those drab impositions of the recent past. Sunglasses, too: the youths whose radios bellowed even as they filed round Sun Yat-sen's memorial in Nanjing were not complete without sunglasses, even though that day the sky was low and the cloud heavy. Jean noticed that it was considered stylish not to remove the small sticky label bearing the manufacturer's name.

In Nanjing zoo there were two Persian cats in a cage, labelled 'Persian cats'. At a commune outside Chengdu they saw a small workshop where fur coats were made from dog-skins; the honeymoon couple dressed up in Alsatian for each other's cameras. At a circus display in Beijing they saw a conjurer juggle with goldfish, producing them with proud aplomb from the baggy sleeves of his silk jacket — a trick which did not seem very difficult to Jean. In Canton, at the Trade Fair, they saw plastic bonsai.

Among the tour guides, it was an indication of status to carry a battery-powered megaphone. At Yangzhou a courier climbed aboard the minibus and welcomed them to the city while the party — none of them more than ten feet from the boomingly amplified voice — quailed in their seats and tried not to laugh. At a jade factory the introductory talk from a forewoman was translated by a guide whose megaphone declined to work. Rather than lay his instrument aside, however, the guide preferred to keep it to his lips and shout through it. At question time, someone asked how you could tell good jade from bad jade. Shouted through the impotent instrument came the reply: 'You look at it and by looking you tell its qualities.'

Jean expected that air travel in China would be blandly international; but even that was quietly Easternized. The air hostesses looked like schoolgirls and didn't seem to know what to do; as they landed in Beijing one of them, she noticed, remained standing all the time and giggled self-consciously when they struck the runway. There was no alcohol served on Chinese airways; instead, you were given bars of Peanut Crisp, pieces of chocolate, packets of sweets, cups of tea and a souvenir. On one flight they gave her a key-ring; on another, a tiny plastic-covered address book whose size suggested that the typical traveller on Chinese airways was a misanthrope.

In Chengdu she asked one of the local guides — a tall, courteous man somewhere between twenty and sixty — about his life. He replied with a mixture of precision and vagueness. He had recently returned from spending ten years in the country. There had been difficulties. He had taught himself English by using records and tapes. Every morning before breakfast he takes the nightsoil to the neighbourhood dump. They have one child. Often the child stays with its grandparents. His wife is a garage mechanic. She works different shifts from him, and this is quite useful as he likes to practise his English with his records and tapes. He does not drink at the banquet in case he disgraces himself and is not invited to join the Party. He wants very much to be invited to join the Party. There have been difficulties but now the difficulties are over. You have one day a week off, plus five days spaced through the year, plus two weeks when you get married. In those two weeks you are allowed to travel. Perhaps people want to divorce so that they get married again and have more holiday.

There were two questions the guide was unable to answer. When Jean asked how much he earned, he seemed — though his English was excellent — not to understand. She repeated the question in more detail, aware that perhaps she was committing a *faux pas*. Eventually, he replied.

'You want to change money?'

Yes, she replied politely, that was what she was trying to ask; perhaps she would be able to change money at the hotel that evening. Perhaps tomorrow would be better, he replied. Of course.

Her other question seemed to her less contentious.

'Do you want to go to Shanghai?'

His expression didn't change; but neither did he reply. Perhaps her pronunciation of the city had been misleading.

'Do you want to go to Shanghai? Shanghai, the big port?'

Again, an attack of temporary deafness. She repeated the question; he merely smiled, and looked around, and didn't reply. Later, thinking the incident over, Jean realized that she hadn't been tactless, as when asking about his income; just inattentive. She had, in fact, already received her answer. He only got single days off; he was married, and had already taken his lifetime's two weeks; you couldn't get to Shanghai and back in a day. Her insertion of the word *want* into the sentence had made it meaningless. What she had been asking was not a real question.

In Nanjing, where it was hot and damp, Jean had experienced her own attack of deafness: she developed a snuffling cold, and one ear refused service. They were staying at a hotel built by an Australian company: a eucalyptus-leaf pattern raged across the bedspread, and koala bears swarmed up the curtains, making her feel even hotter. Half-asleep in the dark, Jean thought she heard a mosquito's thin whine of interest. She wondered why mosquitoes didn't give up on victims who had reached a certain age, and hunt for younger flesh instead; as men did. She pulled the bed-clothes up over her head. After a while this made her too hot; but the moment she gave herself air, the mosquito started up again. Irritated, Jean played this drowsy hide-and-seek a few times, then realized what was happening: the snuffle in her nose, when filtered through her bad ear, was coming out as a mosquito's whine. She woke up completely, checked the genuine silence of the room, and laughed at this little echo from the past. It was just like Sun-Up Prosser: setting off his guns and wheeling about the sky as if attacked. She too was producing her own source of fear, and she too was really quite alone.

*   *   *   *

Aeroplanes — in homage to Prosser she went on calling them aeroplanes long after they had been shortened to planes — never frightened Jean. She didn't need to cram music into her ears through a plastic tube, order stout little bottles of spirits, or probe a heel beneath her seat for the lifejacket. Once she had dropped several thousand feet over the Mediterranean; once her aeroplane had turned back to Madrid and circlingly burnt up fuel for two hours; once, landing from the sea at Hong Kong, they had bounced along the runway like a skimming stone — as if they really had put down on water. But on each occasion Jean had merely withdrawn into thought.

Gregory — studious, melancholy, methodical Gregory — did the worrying for her. When he took Jean to the airport he would smell the kerosene and imagine charred flesh; he would listen to the engines at take-off and hear only the pure voice of hysteria. In the old days, it had been hell, not death, that was feared, and artists had elaborated such fears in panoramas of pain. Now there was no hell, fear was known to be finite, and the engineers had taken over. There had been no deliberate plan, but in elaborating the aeroplane, and in doing all they could to calm those who flew in it, they had created, it seemed to Gregory, the most infernal conditions in which to die.

Ignorance, that was the first aspect of the engineers' modern form of death. It was well known that if anything went wrong with an aeroplane, the passengers were told no more than they needed to know. If a wing fell off, the calm-voiced Scottish captain would tell you that the soft-drinks dispenser was malfunctioning, and this was why he had decided to lose height in a spin without first warning his cargo to put on their seat-belts. You would be lied to even as you died.

Ignorance, but also certainty. As you fell 30,000 feet, whether towards land or water (though water, from that height, would be the same as concrete), you knew that when you hit the ground you would die: you would die, in fact, several hundred times over. Even before the nuclear bomb, the aeroplane had introduced the concept of overkill: as you struck the ground, the jolt from your seat-belt would induce a fatal heart-attack; then fire would burn you to death all over again; then an explosion would scatter you over some forlorn hillside; and then, as rescue teams searched ploddingly for you beneath a mocking sky, the million burnt, exploded, cardiac-arrested bits of you would die once more from exposure. This was normal; this was certain. Certainty ought to cancel out ignorance, but it didn't; indeed, the aeroplane had reversed the established relation between these two concepts. In a traditional death, the doctor at your bedside could tell you what was wrong, but would rarely predict the final outcome: even the most sceptical sawbones had seen a few miracle recoveries. So you were certain of the cause but ignorant of the outcome. Now you were ignorant of the cause but certain of the outcome. This didn't strike Gregory as progress.

Next, enclosure. Do we not all fear the claustrophobia of the coffin? The aeroplane recognized and magnified this image. Gregory thought of pilots in the First World War, the wind playing tunes as it whistled through their struts; of pilots in the Second World War, doing a victory roll and embracing as they did both the skies and the earth. Those fliers touched nature as they moved; and when the plywood biplane peeled apart under sudden air pressure, when the Hurricane, excreting the black smoke of its own obituary, wailed down into some damp cornfield, there was a chance — just a chance — that these endings were in some degree appropriate: the flier had left the earth, and was now being called back. But in a passenger plane with mean windows? How could you feel the dulcet consolation of nature's cycle as you sat there with your shoes off, unable to see out, with your frightened eye everywhere assailed by garish seat-covers? The surroundings were simply not up to it.

And the surroundings included the fourth thing, the company. How would we most like to die? It is not an easy question, but to Gregory there seemed various possibilities: surrounded by your family, with or without a priest — this was the traditional posture, death as a kind of supreme Christmas dinner. Or surrounded by gentle, quiet, attentive medical staff, a surrogate family who knew about relieving pain and could be counted on not to make a fuss. Third, perhaps, if your family failed and you had not merited hospital, you might prefer to die at home, in a favourite chair, with an animal for company, or a fire, or a collection of photographs, or a strong drink. But who would choose to die in the company of three hundred and fifty strangers, not all of whom might behave well? A soldier might charge to a certain death — across the mud, across the veld — but he would die with those he knew, three hundred and fifty men whose presence would induce stoicism as he was sliced in half by machine-gun fire. But these strangers? There would be scream-ing, that much you could rely on. To die listening to your own screams was bad enough; to die listening to the screams of others was part of this new engineers' hell. Gregory imagined himself in a field with a buzzing dot high above. They could all be screaming inside, all three hundred and fifty of them; yet the normal hysteria of the engines would drown everything.

Screaming, enclosed, ignorant and certain. And in addition, it was all so domestic. This was the fifth and final element in the triumph of the engineers. You died with a headrest and an antimacassar. You died with a little plastic fold-down table whose surface bore a circular indentation so that your coffee cup would be held safely. You died with overhead luggage racks and little plastic blinds to pull down over the mean windows. You died with supermarket girls waiting on you. You died with soft furnishings designed to make you feel jolly. You died stubbing out your cigarette in the ashtray on your armrest. You died watching a film from which most of the sexual content had been deleted. You died with the razor towel you had stolen still in your sponge-bag. You died after being told that you had made good time thanks to following winds and were now ahead of schedule. You were indeed: way ahead of schedule. You died with your neighbour's drink spilling over you. You died domestically; yet not in your own home, in someone else's, someone whom you had never met before and who had invited a load of strangers round. How, in such circumstances, could you see your own extinction as something tragic, or even important, or even relevant? It would be a death which mocked you.

*   *   *   *

Jean visited the Grand Canyon in November. The north rim was closed, and the snow-ploughs had been out chivvying the road up from Williams to the south rim. She booked into the lodge at the Canyon's edge; it was early evening. She did not hurry with her unpacking, and even went to the hotel gift shop before looking at the Canyon itself. Not putting off the pleasure, but the reverse; for Jean expected disappointment. At the last minute, she had even considered rescripting her Seven Wonders and visiting the Golden Gate Bridge instead.

A foot of snow lay on the ground and the sun, now almost level with the horizon, had thrown a firm-wristed sweep of orange across the mountains opposite. The sun's kingdom began exactly at the snowline: above, the orange mountain crests had orange snow beneath indolent orange clouds; drop below the line and everything changed into dry browns and buffs and umbers, while far, far down, some murky greens enclosed a trickle of silver — like a lurex thread in a dull tweed suit. Jean gripped the frosty guard-rail and was glad to be alone, glad that what she saw didn't have to be translated into words, to be reported, discussed, annotated. The extravagant fish-eye view was bigger, deeper, wider, grander, savager, more beautiful and more frightening than she had thought possible; but even this alignment of excited adjectives failed her. Rachel, Gregory's

97

most combative girlfriend, had told her before she set off, 'Yeah, it's like coming all the time.' No doubt she'd been trying to shock, and these remembered words were indeed shocking; but only in their inadequacy. Sex — even the resounding sex Jean imagined but had never experienced — could be no more than playing the shoelace game, little tickles on the soles of your feet as the laces snaked away, compared to this. Someone else had promised, 'It's like looking at the Creation' — but that too was only words. Jean was fed up with words. If the Canyon shrank the watchers at its rim to midges, it shrank their noises — the prattle, the whoops, the camera clicks — into mere insect hum. This wasn't a place where you made self-deprecating jokes, fiddled with your exposure meter, or threw snowballs. This was a place beyond words, beyond human noise, beyond interpretation.

It was said that the great Gothic cathedrals of Europe had the power to convert by their mere presence. It wasn't just a question of impressing the peasants: sophisticated minds had also said to themselves, If something as beautiful as this exists, how can the idea which produced it not be true? One cathedral is worth a hundred theologians capable of proving the existence of God by logic. The mind longs for certainty, and perhaps it longs most for a certainty which clubs it down. What the mind can understand, what it can ploddingly prove and approve, might be what it most despises. It longs to be attacked from behind, in a dark street, certainty a knife at the throat.

Perhaps the Canyon acted like a cathedral on religiously inclined tourists, and startlingly argued without words the power of God and the majesty of his works. Jean's response was the opposite. The Canyon stunned her into uncertainty. Over dinner she sat thinking and tried not to use words as she did so; or at least, to use them gingerly. *Therefore* was the word she allowed to set most solid in her mind. The Canyon, *therefore* ... If the Canyon is the question, what is the answer? If the Canyon is the answer, what is the question? The Canyon, *therefore* ... ? Even the sceptic's response, the Canyon, *therefore nothing*, seemed a large answer. It was said that one of the worst tragedies of the spirit was to be born with a religious sense into a world where belief was no longer possible. Was it an equal tragedy to be born without a religious sense into a world where belief *was* possible?

The next morning, before departure, Jean rested her body once more against the frosty guard-rail and gazed at the Canyon. Now the sun was reaching down into it, groping towards the river. High grassy plateaux lay hundreds, perhaps thousands of feet below her. The mountain crests, their soirée of orange glory gone, had become sombre and distant in their morning dress; the snow blinked whitely across. Following its own buzz, a light aeroplane came into view. The first tourist flight of the day, an insect hovering over an enormous wound. For a while it flew level with Jean, then dropped to examine the wandering fissure which enclosed the river. How strange, Jean thought, to stand on the ground and yet be higher than an aeroplane; seeing the wings and fuselage from above was like seeing the rare side of a leaf or a moth. It was somehow against nature, the idea of an aeroplane flying beneath the surface of the earth; as it would be if some surfacing submarine continued to rise out of the water and leaped into the air, a monstrous flying fish.

Against nature. Was that right? We said 'against nature' when we meant 'against reason'. It was nature which provided the miracles, the hallucinations, the beautiful trickery. Forty years ago nature had shown to a Catalina pilot a motor-cyclist calmly riding across the surface of the Atlantic four hundred and fifty miles off the Irish coast. Nature had done that. Reason had subsequently denied the apparition. It was against reason, not against nature. Reason, and man's ingenuity, had erected the first Six Wonders of the World that Jean had visited. Nature had thrown up the seventh, and it was the seventh which had thrown up the questions.

*　　*　　*　　*

Through the RAF Benevolent Fund she traced Sun-Up Prosser's widow. Not Prosser any more, but Redpath, with an address near Whitby. Jean wrote, and a few days later received a post-card of a fishing port under a bright blue sky. 'Pop in any time you're passing. Derek and I like a chat about old times. Fancy Tommy coming up after all this time! P.S. Weather not like on card.'

It was a smart semi-detached council house on a small estate which hadn't yet settled in to the side of a hill; the trees were leafless poles protected by cylinders of wire mesh and the con-crete bus-shelters were still unstained by damp or graffiti. Jean managed to be passing rather sooner than Olive Redpath had anticipated.

'Well, what can it be that's so urgent after it's waited all these years I wonder.' It was half-way between a statement and a question. Jean was handed a cup of coffee and seated in the chair opposite the television. Olive and Derek sat on the divan, Derek behind a vapour trail of cigarette smoke. The divan, Jean noticed, was covered in the sort of bright check material much used for aeroplane seats.

'Oh, it was just that I was, actually, passing. I had to go to Manchester.'

'Manchester. That's passing!' Mrs Redpath cackled at the profligate and impenetrable ways of Southerners. She was stout, bosomy, and aggressively welcoming. 'Hear that, Derek? Man-chester!'

'Surprised you got here safely,' said Derek, taking an un-usually long rest from his cigarette. 'They do say there be canni-bals hereabouts.'

'Well, it's not really urgent, I suppose. It's just that I thought I'd better do it while it was on my mind.'

'Strike while the iron's hot,' said Olive.

'Your . . . your late husband . . . '

'Tommy.'

'Tommy . . . Tommy was billeted on us during the war. With me and my parents. After he was posted from West Malling.

While he was with us we used to talk quite a lot . . . ' She didn't know how to put it exactly.

'One of his popsies, were you?' Olive enquired with a genial laugh.

'No, no, not at all . . . '

'It doesn't bother me if you were, love. I like to think of old Tommy having a last cuddle or two. He always were a bit of a charmer.'

Was he? Jean certainly didn't remember him as a charmer. A bit awkward, fierce, even rude sometimes; capable of being nice. No, charm hadn't seemed one of his components.

'No. I mean, I can see why you might have thought . . . '

'First thing I said, didn't I Derek? Fancy that, I said, one of old Tommy's popsies popping out of the woodwork after all these years. I wouldn't have thrown him out if I'd known.'

'Thrown him out?'

'When we moved, yes, I threw him out. Well, what was the point? When was it, Derek, nine or ten years ago?'

Derek pondered the question as he slowly inhaled and exhaled, then replied, 'It's always longer than you think nowadays.'

'Well, whenever it was, ten or twelve years ago, I threw Tommy out. We were moving, and something had to go, and I hadn't looked at the stuff for years, and his old whatjercallit, battledress or something, I don't know why I had it anyway, it got the moth. So I threw it all out. Letters, photos, a few silly things I didn't look at cause it might upset me. Derek were all in favour.'

'No, that's putting it strong, love.'

'Derek wasn't against, anyway. But what I say is, Tommy's got his little place in my heart, what does he want a place in my attic as well for?' Olive, who had seemed to be moving towards tears, suddenly roared with laughter, her motion shaking some ash from Derek's cigarette. 'He was a lovely boy, from what I remember of him, Tommy. But then life must go on, mustn't it?'

'Yes,' said Jean.

'Quicker than you think,' put in Derek.

'Not that I'd have thought you were his type,' Olive said quizzically.

'Oh, I wasn't,' said Jean. There was a pause. 'I was wondering ... We lost touch with him when he was posted. I was wondering ... when he was with us he was so keen to get back to flying.'

'Was he?' said Olive. 'I always thought he had a bit of a yellow streak in him myself.' She noticed the change in Jean's expression. 'You sure you weren't one of his popsies? You're behaving as if you were. No, I'm only trying to say what I mean. No point doing otherwise, is there?'

'No,' replied Jean. 'I wasn't shocked. I just thought he was brave. I thought they were all brave.'

'Well, Tommy P. had one eye open for the back door, if you catch my drift. Not that I ever held it against him. That's why I was a bit surprised when I heard he'd gone back to flying.'

'He always seemed so keen to.'

'So you say. Well, you do surprise me. Still, we can't settle it now, and I haven't got his letters since I threw him out.' Olive chuckled. 'Anyway, I was a bit more surprised than you must have been. And then, let me see ...' She paused, even though she must have told the story many times before. 'It can only have been a few days after that, a week maybe, and I got a letter from his squadron thingy ...'

'Leader,' Derek supplied.

'... leader, thank you, saying he was missing, believed killed in action. I was a bit of a heap at that, I don't mind telling you. I mean, I was really soft on Tommy, only been married a year or so, going to start a family as soon as the war was over ... So I wrote to the squadron thingy and said, What action? Killed in what action? And he wrote and said he was sorry all over again, and said Tommy was a wonderful fellow, though how he can have known that seeing as Tommy had only been posted a few days, and then something about security reasons or whatever. I wrote back and said, That's not good enough, I want to know and I'm coming to see you. And before he could write back and say *that* was against security thingies I set off. More coffee, love?'

'No thanks.'

'The Cona's on, so just say. Well, I got there, which wasn't easy, and I saw the squadron fellow and said, Listen, what action? Killed in what action? Where? He was nice enough, but said he couldn't tell me. I said who do you think I am, Lord Haw-Haw? My Tommy's been killed and I want to know where. And eventually he said France, and I said well that narrows it down I thought it might be Iceland. And anyway what do you mean, missing and killed? If he's missing maybe he isn't killed, and if he's killed he isn't missing, is he? So the squadron fellow said that Tommy had got, what was the word, detached from the rest of the fellows — I said that was just like him, going off on his own — and that a bit later one of the other pilots had seen a Hurricane coming down out of control and he went to take a look and it was Tommy, and this other fellow watched it and it went down and hit the ground.

'So I said, I want to talk to this fellow. He said it was against regulations but I carried on like a woman for a bit, said I'd sit in his office till I got what I wanted and so on, wept buckets — well, that wasn't hard, and do you know what he said?'

'He said you'd have to sign the Official Secrets Act,' put in Derek.

'I know *you* know, stupid. So I said that's all right by me. Get them out. So I signed whatever it was, could have been signing for dentures for all I knew, and they took me to this fellow. Mac something, I don't remember. But the squadron fellow had obviously given him a talking-to beforehand. He just said over France, going down. I said how did you know it was Tommy? He said there were numbers on the side of the aeroplane. Went past nice and slow, did it, so that you could read them, I said. He said the numbers were painted big so you could read them, but he could see I was upset. I was crying again, and all I could think of was how big the numbers were. And then this Mac fellow stood up and shook my hand and said that was all he knew but if I happened to be in the Three Ships at about eight he might just have remembered a bit more.

'I was in the pub at opening time, I don't mind telling you. I might even have been a bit whistled by the time he turned up; but I remember everything he said. They were over France, about eight of them, and they noticed that Tommy was sort of drifting away. Looking for the back door, I wouldn't have been surprised. So the fellow in charge calls him up on the whatsit . . .'

'Radio,' murmured Derek, helping, not answering.

'. . . radio and told him to get back in line. There wasn't any reply. He tried several times, but it looked as if Tommy's radio wasn't working. Then they noticed he was beginning to climb away from them, and the fellow in charge told this Mac to go and see if he could catch him up. He said it wasn't easy because Tommy seemed to be climbing straight into the sun, and you couldn't see too much. But after a bit he got near enough to see that Tommy was still there — he hadn't fainted or anything. He had his hand up in front of his face. It must have been so that he wasn't blinded by the sun. That's what they did, this Mac said, when they were climbing into the sun. So he tried talking to Tommy on the radio, but he wouldn't answer. He fired his guns, but that didn't work either.

'So the fellow in charge told him to get back and join the others, and let Tommy do whatever was in his sweet mind to do. I mean, it sounds like his plane had gone wrong, doesn't it, and he couldn't stop it going up? So Mac sets off to rejoin the others, and when he's half-way there he sees this Hurricane coming down in a dive. I said, that's when you read the numbers. He looked a bit shamefaced, and said the aeroplane was out of control, and he didn't see the numbers, but when it was sort of level with him, he could see the pilot. Well, he could see the outline of the pilot. He obviously couldn't tell that it was Tommy, but he said whoever it was had their hand held up in front of their eyes like Tommy had when he was climbing. And then Mac followed him down for a bit, but there wasn't any chance. And there wasn't a parachute either. And that was my Tommy gone.'

Derek put his arm round Olive and cuddled her, the smoke from his cigarette curling up her shoulder and drifting into her hair.

Jean didn't know what to say; she sat and waited.

'Do you remember him well?' Olive eventually asked.

'Yes,' said Jean, 'I remember him well. I was quite young at the time. He . . . he used to make me All-Clear sandwiches.'

Olive didn't respond to this. 'Did you notice the way he always had the top button of his tunic undone?'

'No, I don't think I did.'

'Did you notice the way he was always looking round — couldn't keep his head still?'

'Yes, I remember that.' Michael had commented on it, had used it to prove that Prosser was shifty. 'I assumed he had a twitch or something.'

'Twitch?' said Olive crossly. 'No bloody twitch. Listen, love, if you were flying one of those Hurricanes you had to turn your head every three seconds or you were dead.' In the cardiganed nook of Derek's shoulder, Olive turned her head from side to side, squinting into the sun for a Messerschmidt. 'You got into the habit, you see.'

'I see.'

'That's why he always had the top button of his tunic undone. You were allowed that because you had to turn your head so much. It was a privilege. They allowed you that.' Olive continued to turn her head from side to side, stopping only to take a draw from Derek's cigarette.

'I see.'

'No one understood Tommy like I did,' said Olive rather fiercely, and Derek cuddled her in silence.

On the train home, Jean stared out of the window and thought about Sun-Up Prosser's last flight. It could have been a technical fault, of course: he might have got stuck in a climb; he might have been so busy trying to control the aeroplane that he couldn't answer the R/T or the other pilot's guns. But she doubted this. It all sounded too close to what she'd once heard him say, forty years earlier. Climbing into the sun, watching it through slightly parted fingers. The air getting thinner; the aeroplane skidding about and climbing more slowly. The patch of frost forming inside the Perspex hood. The gathering cold. The thinning oxygen. The gradual invasion of contentment, then of joy. The slowness; the happy slowness of it all . . .

*   *   *   *

When Jean gave birth to Gregory, when she suckled him, when she despatched him to school, when she stood on the zig-zag fire-escape outside Towcester and watched his Vampire glide gently down while its engine plumed off in pointless acceleration, she had all the normal wishes for her son. May you do well, may you be happy, may you be healthy, may you be intelligent, may you be loved; may you love me. As he bent patiently over a latticework of aeroplane struts, as he dampened the tissue-paper and waited for time to pull it taut, as he filled the room with pear-drops, she idly constructed her own images, the accepted ways in which each generation sees its relationship to the next. They stand on our shoulders, she thought, and with the added height they can see farther. They can also, from up there, look back at the path we have taken and avoid making the mistakes we did. We are handing something on to them — a torch, a relay baton, a burden. As we weaken, they grow strong: the young man carries the ancestor on his back and leads his own child by the hand.

But she had also seen enough to doubt all this. These images appeared strong, but they were made only of balsa wood and tissue-paper. As often as not the parent stands on the child's shoulders, crushing it into the soft soil. The child sees all too well the parent's mistakes, but learns only to make quite different mistakes. The parent indeed hands something on to the child: haemophilia, syphilis, hay fever. The ancestor dutifully loaded on the back causes a slipped disc, the child in the hand a wrenched shoulder. And so Jean also wished for her son the negative things, the avoidances. May you avoid misery, poverty, disease. May you be unremarkable. May you do the best you can but not chase impossibilities. May you be safe within yourself. May you not get burnt, even once.

In later years she wondered if these wan ambitions had communicated themselves to Gregory. If the child in the uterus can sense and be damaged by parental arguments, how much more likely that the born child can absorb silent hopes — hopes which hang in the air as heavy as the smell of pear-drops. Was it perhaps Jean's doing that Gregory became a wary, unrebellious adolescent, and later a withdrawn young man? He was polite and presentable; no one objected to his roundish, pinkish face, to the schoolmasterly look his horn-rimmed glasses gave him; yet occasionally Jean caught herself thinking, you could be anyone else. You could. You could be someone who wasn't my son at all. But this, she realized, was roughly what she had hoped for him in the first place. May you be unremarkable. May you not chase impossibilities.

Her more spoken hopes for Gregory went like this. Don't settle your life too soon. Don't do something at twenty which will tie you down for the rest of your life. Don't do what I did. Travel. Enjoy yourself. Find out who and what you are. Explore.

Gregory understood his mother's urgings, but felt, as children do, that they were really back-dated wishes for the parent rather than pertinent hopes for the child. True, he didn't want to tie himself down; but he didn't much want to travel. True, he wanted to find out who he was, whatever that meant; but he wanted to do it without exploring much. Enjoy himself? Yes, he wanted to enjoy himself. Or rather, he wanted to want to enjoy himself. The rest of the world, it seemed to Gregory, had a much securer hold on pleasure than he did. They saw what it was, did what was required to have it, and had it. How could they know in advance where pleasure lay? Presumably, they examined other people, noted what they enjoyed, did the same, and had enjoyment themselves. To Gregory things did not seem so simple. When he examined groups of people intent on pleasure — pub drinkers, sports fans, seaside bathers — he felt crisp envy, but also furtive embarrassment. Perhaps some dislocation had taken place inside him. Pleasure, he was aware, could be obtained only if you believed in pleasure. The pilot at the end of the runway believes in flight. It's not just a question of knowledge, of understanding aerodynamics; it's also a question of belief. Gregory would sit shuddering on the tarmac; the tower would give him the off; but half-way down the runway he always jammed on the brakes. He didn't believe this kite could fly.

He had girlfriends, but he found, when he was with them, that he never felt quite what he was expected to feel: the inaccessibility of group pleasure, he realized, could even extend to gatherings of two. Sex didn't make him feel lonely; but it didn't, on the other hand, make him feel particularly accompanied. As for male camaraderie, there often seemed something false about it. Groups of men got together because they feared complications. They wanted to make things simpler for themselves; they wanted certainty; they wanted definite rules. Look at monasteries. Look at pubs.

Gregory didn't travel, nor did he marry. For most of his life he lived near Jean, which she at first tried to discourage but later accepted as a pale compliment. Gregory tried various jobs in the first years of adulthood, but concluded that one was much the same as another. All jobs were boring, but you had to have one, because the point of a job was to make you value the time when you were away from it. When he told people this, they thought he was being cynical, but he wasn't. It just seemed obvious. Life depended on contrasts, and continued to do so until you ran into the ultimate contrast.

Gregory worked in an insurance office. He liked the job because people asked him little about it. They would observe that they were sure it was interesting work, and he would nod, and they would ask if they could take out a policy against it raining on their holidays, and he would say yes they could, and they would laugh and say fancy that, then seem to run out of interest. This suited Gregory.

It also suited him to be dealing with life insurance. When he took it up he had not yet come to the conclusion that life was absurd – he was still weighing this up – but he had certainly decided that your job ought to be absurd. The concept of 'useful work', which politicians dealt in, made no sense to Gregory. It seemed to him that work was useful only to the extent that it was useless, that it mocked itself. Painting the Forth Bridge sounded an excellent job, because no sooner had you finished than you had to start again. Life insurance could not aspire to such a perfection of irony, but it had its aptness. Gregory particularly enjoyed telling people how much they got if they died. He relished the greed and calculation on their faces: all this money they would get in exchange for such a simple thing as being dead. Once he was explaining a policy to a man in his mid-twenties — such and such payable per month, this much on death, this much on maturation of the policy — when he was interrupted.

'So if I sign this today, and I die tomorrow, then I get £25,000?'

At first Gregory was professionally suspicious of the man's enthusiasm. He explained about paying the initial premium, about the policy's invalidity in case of suicide or concealment of serious illness . . .

'Yes, yes, yes,' said the man impatiently. 'But if I'd paid up, and if *quite by accident*' – he stressed this enthusiastically – 'I went under a bus tomorrow, I'd get £25,000?'

'Yes.' Gregory didn't like to point out that it was the man's widow or parents or whoever that would actually get the money. It seemed almost in bad taste to do so.

But this was why he liked life insurance. Of course there was much euphemism involved, much disguise of a policy as a pension; but when it came down to it what people were trying to do was get the best deal they could out of being dead. People — the sort of people he dealt with — had been educated in thrift; they had been taught to shop around; and they applied their normal commercial senses to the largest matters as well. Even those who admitted that they themselves would not actually get the money could still be entranced by the transaction. Death may come and steal me away, but oh boy, what a daft move it is on his part, because it leaves the wife rolling in money. If only Death had realized *that*, he wouldn't have been so greedy.

Life insurance. Even the phrase was a glowing oxymoron. Life. You couldn't insure it, ensure it, assure it; but people thought they could. They sat across the desk from Gregory and weighed up the advantages of their own extinction. Sometimes he thought he didn't understand people at all. They were on such shoulder-rubbing terms with everything: they were greasily familiar with pleasure, they hob-nobbed and bargained with death. They didn't seem at all surprised to be alive in the first place; once here, they made the best of it; and when departing, they struck the best deal they could. How strange. How admirable, he supposed, but how strange.

Other people's lives, deaths and pleasures: they seemed increasingly mysterious to Gregory. He peered out at them through his horn-rimmed spectacles and wondered why they did the things they did. Perhaps they did such things — ordinary things — because they didn't bother too much with the why or the how; perhaps Gregory was hobbled by thought. His mother, for instance: look at the way she had suddenly started travelling all over the world. If you asked her why, she'd smile and say something about ticking off the Seven Wonders. But that wasn't *why*. And yet *why* didn't seem to bother her.

Gregory had never wanted to travel; perhaps being carted around England at an early age had something to do with it. He made the occasional trip, never more than a hundred miles or so, to see what life was like away from where he lived. It seemed very much the same. Travel made you tired, it made you fretful, it flattered you. People said that travel broadened the mind. Gregory didn't believe this. What it did was give the illusion of broadening the mind. For Gregory, what broadened the mind was staying at home.

When he thought of travel, he also remembered Cadman the Aviator. In Shrewsbury, at the church of St Mary's, Gregory had come across a commemorative tablet. The full circumstances of Cadman's flight were not explained, but it appeared that in 1739 this modern Icarus had built himself a pair of wings, climbed to the top of the church and jumped off. He died, of course. The pilot error of pride; but also, as with Icarus, a technical fault:

> 'Twas not for want of skill;
> Or Courage, to perform the task, he fell;
> No, no — a faulty cord, being drawn too tight,
> Hurry'd his soul on high to take her flight,
> Which bid the body here beneath, good night.

Occasionally, when he saw Jean off at some airport, Gregory would think of Cadman. One of the first modern aeroplane crashes. Fatalities 100 per cent — the usual ratio. Cadman didn't lack courage (the plaque was right), just brains. Gregory imagined trying to work out the Aviator's chances of survival. No, he definitely wouldn't have been allowed to sell him a life insurance policy.

But there was something else about Cadman. Apart from the manner of death, Gregory remembered the epitaph's poetic argument. The Aviator was seeking to fly and failed; but while his body fell and was crushed, his soul rose and flew instead. It was, no doubt, a moral lesson about ambition and human conceit: if God had intended us to fly, he would have given us wings. But did not the story also imply that God rewarded the brave by giving them eternal life? If so — if Heaven was gained by courage — then Gregory didn't rate his chances.

He recalled a scene from his childhood. Launching a model aeroplane from ... not a church tower, but a flat roof or something. He'd obviously failed to attach the engine properly to the fuselage, because the jet had torn itself loose. The aeroplane had fallen down, like Cadman's body, while the engine had screamed off up the garden like Cadman's soul on its way to Heaven.

Is this how people — the people who smiled shyly across his desk when he mentioned thousands of pounds — thought of death? Gregory imagined a more public version of his own back-garden experiment: a space launch. The huge, lumbering rocket, like the body, and the tiny capsule on top of it, like the soul. The body packed with enough fuel to enable the soul to outsoar the lapping gravity of the earth. If you looked at the fat carrot on the launch-pad, you might think the rocket the important part, but it wasn't. The rocket was disposable, like Cadman's body; it was merely there to launch the soul.

Gregory puzzled with these images for a while, before remembering the end of his Vampire's flight. Jean had found its engine in the ginger beech hedge at the bottom of the garden. Argument? Perhaps the soul does outsoar the body, but only for a certain time, a certain distance. The soul might be superior to the body without being as different from it as people imagined. The soul might be made of a more durable material — aluminium as against balsa wood, say — but one which would eventually prove just as susceptible to time and space and gravity as did poor Cadman's body, or his own gold-painted Vampire.

*   *   *   *

Rachel had always seemed the least probable of Gregory's girlfriends. He was passive by nature, and left little trace of himself on the world. Jean sometimes thought that if you covered his fingertips with aeroplane glue, you could peel away a set of prints with scarcely a whorl. Faint in personality, he normally went for even fainter, more passive girls: girls with transparent skins and a defeated manner. Rachel was small and fierce, with swivelling brown eyes and short, tightly curled blond hair of the sort Jean imagined you might get on some rare brand of mountain sheep. Rachel not only knew her own mind, she knew other people's as well, especially Gregory's. Jean had heard about the attraction of opposites, but still did not give the relationship long.

The first time Gregory brought Rachel home there was an argument about lavatory seats. This, at any rate, was how Jean remembered the occasion; though Rachel, who had debated as if the Battle of Britain might turn on the skirmish, later claimed not to remember the discussion. It was one of those rows which came from nowhere — the normal source of rows, according to Jean. After living with Michael, she felt she had had enough of them for a lifetime. But nowadays women seemed to be starting more than they used to. And Rachel worked in one of these neighbourhood law centres; weren't they meant to help keep the peace?

'Well, what about lavatory seats?' this girl suddenly shouted at Gregory, her brown eyes opening wider, her hair seeming to bristle. Jean could have been mistaken, but didn't think the matter had come up before. 'Who do you think they're designed for?'

'Oh, people,' replied Gregory with a pedantic and, as his mother thought, rather charming half-smile.

'Men,' Rachel had explained, slowing the vowel with condescending patience. 'Meeeeen.'

'I didn't know you had any . . . trouble,' said Gregory, sensing perhaps that an entirely pacific response would cause more irritation. 'I mean, has someone had to pull you out?'

'When I sit there,' this surprising creature announced, 'I think, this was made for men by other men. What do you think?' She turned to Jean.

'I don't honestly think about it, I'm afraid.' Her tone was vague rather than prim.

'Well, there you are,' commented Gregory with an unwise complacency.

'There you are, there you aren't,' shouted Rachel, preferring vigour of argument to immediate logic. 'Steps,' she said. 'Step-ladders as well. Getting off trains. Pedals on a car. The Stock Exchange.'

Gregory laughed. 'You can't expect . . . '

'Why not? Why not? Why shouldn't *you* learn? Why is it

always us? What about changing a wheel? Why are the nuts screwed on so bloody hard that a woman can't bloody shift them?'

'Because if they weren't your bloody wheels would bloody fall off.'

But Rachel was undeterred. 'Headrests,' she continued. 'Judges. Printers. Taxi-drivers. Motor-mowers. *Language*.'

Jean found herself chuckling.

'What are you laughing at? It's worse for you.'

'Why is it worse for me?'

'Because you grew up not knowing it.'

'I don't think you know me quite well enough to say that.' Jean liked Rachel's unselfconsciousness, and her confidence. 'No, I wasn't laughing at you, dear. I was thinking about the Stock Exchange.'

'What about it?'

'Well, when I was a child I remember being warned against the Stock Exchange. It was put on a level with gambling and swindling and going on strike.'

'You don't take things seriously,' said Rachel crossly. 'You ought to take things seriously.'

'Well,' said Jean, trying to take things seriously, 'perhaps it's a good idea for women to . . . to adapt. Perhaps it makes their minds more flexible. Perhaps we ought to be sorry for men. The way they can't adapt.'

'That's a man's argument.'

'Is it? Isn't it just an argument?'

'No, it's a man's argument. It's one of those they handed to us because they knew it wouldn't work. Like giving us a set of spanners that don't fit the nuts.'

'Perhaps that's why you can't change a wheel,' said Gregory, smiling to himself.

'Fuck off, Gregory.'

Yes, thought Jean. I don't give this more than a few weeks. On the other hand, I do rather like her.

They visited Jean several more times, and on each occasion

Gregory seemed a little less there; the presence of this forceful girl rendered him almost translucent. Rachel increasingly addressed her remarks to Jean. One afternoon, when Gregory had made some unappreciated joke about lavatory seats and disappeared, Rachel said quietly, 'Come to a film tomorrow.'

'I'd love to.'

'And . . . don't tell Gregory.'

'All right.'

How strange, Jean thought the next morning, to be going out with her own son's girlfriend. Well, 'going out' was probably the wrong phrase for the cinema and a Chinese meal. But even so, she felt excited and fussed about her clothes until she began to embarrass herself. 'I'll pick you up at seven,' Rachel had said, quite naturally; and the words had echoed strangely for Jean. That was what the young men in Austin Sevens, the courtiers with motor-bike and sidecar, were supposed to have said. The suitors she had never had, forty years ago. Now the words were finally uttered by a girl, someone less than half her age.

The film, which Rachel had chosen, was harsh, Germanic and political; even the moments of tenderness in it were swiftly revealed to be illusory or manipulative. Jean disliked it strongly, but also found it completely interesting. This sort of response was something she increasingly noticed. Previously — a word which covered all her life — she had been interested in what she liked, and not interested in what she disliked; more or less, anyway. She had assumed everyone was like this. But a new layer of responsiveness seemed to have grown; now she was sometimes bored by what she approved of, and could sympathize with what she disapproved of. She wasn't entirely sure how beneficial this development was; but the fact that it was taking place was undeniable, and surprising.

Rachel had paid for Jean's cinema ticket, and also let her know she would be paying for dinner.

'But I've got some money.' Jean began to dig in her handbag while the waiter had still to take their order. She pulled out some five-pound notes crumpled into balls. This was how she carried money, as it reduced the vague shame attached to producing it. Screw the notes up and they could be used, or discussed, without too much embarrassment.

Rachel leaned across the table, folded Jean's hands round the money and pushed it back into the bag. Among the fluff and make-up at the bottom, a dull glint read: JEAN SERJEANT XXX.

'You're not out with a man now,' said Rachel.

Jean smiled. Of course she wasn't. And yet, in a curious way, she was. Or, more exactly, she was behaving as if she was. The care she'd taken with her clothes; the way she hadn't quite said what she thought about the film as they left the cinema; her air of subordination to Rachel when they got to the restaurant. Perhaps it was just age's deference to youth; perhaps not. 'But you've made me put my money away,' she said. 'That's what men do.'

'Not any more.'

'Don't they?'

'No. Nowadays they take half your money and then still treat you the way they used to when they paid for everything.'

'Which is?'

'Tell me about China.' On the restaurant wall was a boxed colour slide of an idealized Eastern landscape: a cascading river, emerald trees, a Hollywood sky. By some primitive process of animation the river flashed and glinted, while the clouds clumped slowly sideways. 'Well, it wasn't like that,' Jean said. Wryly noting Rachel's imperiousness, she began, as her mother would have put it, to sing for her supper.

They talked about China and travel, then about friendship and marriage. Jean found it easy to discuss her life with Michael, noting the flares of retrospective anger in her young friend, but continuing as calmly as possible. At the end, Rachel said, 'I can't understand why you stayed. Why it lasted.'

'Oh, the usual reasons. Fear. Fear of loneliness. Money. Not wanting to admit that you'd failed.'

'No, *you* didn't fail. If *you* left, *he* failed; that's what they don't understand.'

'Perhaps. And there were other reasons. After I married I lost a lot of confidence. I didn't understand things. I was always wrong. I didn't know the answers. I didn't even know the questions. But after a while — five years or so — it began to change. I was unhappy, and bored too, I expect, but all the time I seemed to be understanding more about things. About the world. The more unhappy I became, the more intelligent I felt.'

'Haven't you got it the wrong way round — the more intelligent you became, the more unhappy you felt because you'd been conned?'

'Perhaps. I don't know. But I started to get superstitious about it. I can't leave, I thought, because if I become less unhappy, I'll become less intelligent as well.'

'And did you, when you left?'

'No, but that's not the point. And there's another reason which I'm sure you'll think is just as silly. I probably won't be able to explain it very well; but I remember when it happened. Michael and I wouldn't be speaking much; he'd be angry, I'd be bored; sometimes he'd be drinking, and occasionally I'd disappear, just to make him worry about me, or try to make him worry about me. If it was warm I'd sometimes spend the whole evening in the garden, just so as not to be with him.

'Anyway, that sort of time. Not much fun. I was sitting in the garden one night. The house was blacked-out, like in the war. There wasn't any cloud, just one of those special moons as bright as the Arctic sun. A bombers' moon, we used to call it . . . And I suddenly thought, what's it for, this marriage? Why stay? Why not slip away into the warm night? And perhaps it was lack of sleep, and I felt a bit light-headed, but the answer seemed obvious. I stay because everything says I should go, because it doesn't make sense, because it's absurd. Like whoever it was said they believed in God because it was absurd. I really understood that.'

'I don't,' said Rachel. 'And I hope I never do.'

'Don't count on it. It can be very tiring being rational all the time.'

'But that's why I like you,' said Rachel. 'Because you're never silly.'

Jean smiled and looked down. She felt a cautious pleasure. 'That's very sweet of you. People always assume that by the time you reach my age you don't need compliments any more. The old need them just as much as the young.'

'You're not old,' said Rachel, fiercely.

'Oh dear. Another compliment. Oh dear.' She liked Rachel, but was a little frightened of her. The certainty, and the crossness. Years ago, it had only been men who had been so certain and so cross.

That was really why she had gone to live on her own. Marriage had two magnetic poles, anger and fear. But now women were getting just as good at anger. It puzzled Jean that it was often the women who rejected men most thoroughly, who went off and lived with one another, who announced their freedom from the sovereignty of the opposite sex, that seemed to be the angriest. Shouldn't they be the calmest, now that they had got what they wanted? Or was it part of some wider rage against a created world which only offered two choices, one of them pitiably inadequate? Jean didn't feel she could ask Rachel, because it would only make her cross. That was another thing: women were angry with other women nowadays. In Asian times, in that old world where men bullied and women deceived themselves, where hypocrisy was used like camomile lotion, there had at least been some sly complicity among women, all women. Now there was acceptable thinking, loyalty and betrayal. That's what it seemed like to Jean. But perhaps you could learn only so much in your life. Your tanks held only so much fuel, and she was losing height. The lower you got, the less you saw.

'Do you mind if I ask you about sex? I mean ... ' For once, Rachel hesitated.

'No, of course not, dear. It did go on all those years ago, surprising as it might seem.'

'Was it ... Was it ... ' Again, Rachel seemed uncertain. 'Was it all right?'

Jean laughed. She picked up a blue teacup, made of some unknown material half-way between china and plastic, hesitated, sipped, and listened to the odd, cracked noise it made when she placed it on the saucer.

'When I was in China they had just announced a new Marriage Act. I remember reading a translation. It was very full, it covered almost everything. It said you couldn't marry if one partner had leprosy, and it said that infanticide by drowning was strictly prohibited. I remember going through it wondering what the Party had laid down about sex. I mean, it lays down everything about everything on the whole. All it had was Article 12.' She paused, rather needlessly.

'I can't be expected to guess.'

. 'No. Article 12 reads: "Husband and wife are in duty bound to practise family planning".' She paused again, this time more meaningly.

'So?'

'Well, I suppose you could say we had a Chinese marriage. It was more a matter of practising family planning than, what do you say nowadays, having sex.'

'I think that's sad.'

'There are worse things. We weren't the only ones. There were lots of Chinese marriages then. I expect there still are. It didn't seem so ... important. There was a war, and then there was peace, and things like ... ' she found herself stuck for an example, ' ... things like the Festival of Britain ... '

'Oh for Christ's sake.'

'I'm sorry. But it's the sort of thing I mean. We didn't think nothing else mattered. We didn't ... '

'Will you go to bed with me?' Rachel asked it quickly, head down, her curly hair pointed at Jean.

'Well, dear, it's very sweet of you, but I'm an old lady ... '

'Don't patronize me. And don't patronize yourself.' Rachel was frowning fiercely. Jean still declined to take her seriously.

'Just because you buy me dinner ... '

'I mean it.'

Suddenly Jean felt much older than this girl, and a bit fed up with her. 'Come on, we're going now,' she said. 'Pay the bill.'

But in the car she rested her hand on Rachel's shoulder. They drove in silence for a while, with Rachel occasionally swearing at male drivers. Eventually, without looking across at Jean, she said, 'I'm not as crude as you think, you know.'

'I didn't say you were.'

'With Gregory, I mean. There's just something about him that gets on my tits.'

'Well then, you're better off without him.'

'He never thinks about being a man. I don't mean *being a man*, climbing mountains and that. I just mean just being a man. He doesn't think about that. Most of them don't, and Gregory's no better than the rest of them. He just thinks he's the norm.'

'I think Gregory's rather a sensitive boy.'

'I'm not saying that, I'm not saying *that*. It's just that he thinks being a man is the norm. He thinks you and me belong to a deviant species.'

'Are you saying it's because of the way I brought him up?'

'No, I mean, Christ, if there'd been a man around the place he'd probably have been a lot worse.'

'Thanks for the compliment,' said Jean ruefully. They drove on while the night's clouds oozed drizzle on to the car.

'The thing about being on the pill,' said Rachel suddenly, 'is that you can fuck people you don't like.'

'Why ever would you want to do that?'

Silence. Oh dear. Wrong again. She'd asked another question that wasn't a real question. How much do you earn? Do you want to go to Shanghai?

'When Michael died,' Jean said, without knowing what had brought the subject into her head, 'he left me all his money. The house. Everything.'

'Of course he did,' said Rachel crossly. 'The shit. Big daddy. Make you feel grateful.'

This didn't seem good enough to Jean. 'But what would you have said if he'd left me nothing?'

In the half-light of the car Jean saw Rachel smile. 'I'd have said, the shit. Big daddy. Took the best twenty years of your life and still wanted to punish you and make you feel guilty at the end.'

'In fact,' said Jean, 'he didn't leave a will. Or at least, not one they found. He died intestate. So Gregory and I got everything. What do you make of that?'

Rachel was almost laughing with crossness. 'The shit. Big daddy. Couldn't decide whether to make you feel guilty or grateful. Wanted to have it both ways, even when he was dying. Wanted to make sure you carried on trying to work it out for years afterwards. Typical.'

'So he couldn't win?'

'Not in my eyes. In his eyes he wins every way round.'

'I used to think I knew the answers,' said Jean. 'That's why I left. I know what to do, I thought. Perhaps you have to persuade yourself you know the answers otherwise you don't ever do anything. I thought I knew the answers when I married — or at least, I thought I was going to find them out. I thought I knew the answers when I left. Now I'm not sure. Or rather, I know the answers to different things now. Perhaps that's it: we're only capable of knowing the answers to a certain number of things at any particular time.'

'You see,' said Rachel. 'He's still got you thinking about him. The shit.'

As they drew up outside Jean's house, Rachel began again. 'I went out with someone once. He was good company, clever, nice enough; he wasn't too bad for a man. It was all right. Until I caught him watching me as I came.'

'You mean . . . from the window?'

'No, Jean, not from the window.' Oh dear, thought Jean, we're still on that. 'Not from the window. In bed. Sex. Fucking.'

'Yes.'

'He used to watch me. Like I was a performing animal. How's it getting on down there? Out of the corner of his eye. It was

121

creepy. I decided to pay him back. I got a bit obsessed by it. I mean, I could see the relationship didn't have far to go, but I really wanted to pay him back. Make him remember me.

'I began to fake not coming. Does that shock you?' Jean shook her head. My, how things had changed. Rachel went on; her tone was aggressive, but Jean heard an edge of uncertainty in it. 'It was quite hard at first, and sometimes I failed, but I did it enough times. And it really got to him. First I'd come, but pretend not to, and then I'd make him go on and on, and I'd pretend I was just over the horizon, not much further, just round the next bend, you know. And then I'd let him off, like a schoolboy. No, it's all right, it doesn't matter. And then, when he'd rolled off and was almost asleep but not quite, I'd pretend to help myself along a bit. Nothing dramatic, just enough to let him know I was doing it and pretending to keep quiet so as not to hurt his feelings. That really got to him. Quite a lot. The shit.'

Why go to all that trouble, Jean thought as she got out of the car. First to do it, and then to tell me. Unless . . . it wasn't about Gregory, was it? She tried to remember her worst times with Michael: dull days beneath an angry sky, lonely nights beneath a bombers' moon. She had been sad, disappointed, angry; but couldn't remember anything near the contempt that Rachel had just exhibited. Was this a matter of character or generation? People were always saying that women had more freedom, more money, more choices now. Perhaps such advances couldn't be obtained without a necessary toughening of character. This would explain why things often seemed worse, not better, between the sexes; why there was so much aggression, and why they were so pleased to call aggression honesty. Or perhaps, Jean thought, perhaps there is a simpler explanation: I have forgotten how I felt. The mind has a way of putting unhelpful memories down its waste-disposal unit. Forgetting yesterday's fear ensures today's survival. When I was living with Michael I might have felt such anger and contempt, but I stifled them with a pillow like two squeaking puppies, and now I can no longer recall where I buried the bodies.

Rachel said: 'I love the fear in a man's eye when he meets an intelligent woman.' Rachel said: 'If there's one thing I despise it's a man who sucks up to women.' Rachel said: 'Only a woman can understand a woman.' She had left home at sixteen, drifted round several large cities, lived for a time in houses from which men were excluded. Rachel said: 'Men are beating up women more than they ever used to. Men are killing children.' Rachel said: 'What's the difference between a man and a turd? You don't have to hug a turd after you've laid it.' Rachel said: 'It's all about money and politics, don't ever imagine that it isn't.' Rachel said: 'I'm not criticizing, I just think you're still hoping for some man to come along and answer all the questions for you.'

Jean pictured a seesaw, painted municipal green, in a council playground. A fat man in a three-piece suit was sitting on one end, weighing it down. Precariously, Jean climbed on and took the first seat opposite him; but her small weight, placed so close to the fulcrum, made no impact. Rachel arrived, monkey-crawled to the highest point of the seesaw, way beyond Jean, and there, with no thought for her safety or the asphalt below, began jumping up and down. The fat man in the business suit looked briefly discommoded, then shifted on his haunches and settled himself again; his heels hadn't even lifted from the ground. After a while, Rachel left in disgust. Later, and more cautiously, Jean in turn slipped down and went away. The fat man didn't seem in the least upset. Somebody else would be along quite soon. Besides, he owned the playground.

Rachel said: '*Three* wise men — are you serious?' Rachel said: 'If they can put one man on the moon, why don't they put them all there?' Rachel said: 'A woman needs a man like a tree needs a dog with a lifted leg.' Rachel had once been given her father's shoes to clean and instead of using polish had smeared them with toothpaste; she had watched her mother's intelligence being frittered away on calculations about the price of tinned food; she had watched her father hold her mother in the soft cage of his hands. Rachel said: 'A man on a white charger is all very well, but who's going to clear up the droppings?' Rachel said: 'Being born a woman is being born left-handed and forced to write with the other one. No wonder we stammer.' Rachel said: 'You think I'm shouting? You don't know how deaf they are.'

Jean found herself wondering if Rachel's father had maltreated her, if there had been some scarring first involvement with a man; but Rachel guessed her thought before she had begun it. 'Jean,' she said, 'that's a man's argument. The spanner doesn't fit the nut.' 'I just wondered . . .' said Jean. 'Well, stop. You don't have to have been raped to be a feminist. You don't have to look like a garage mechanic. You just have to be normal. You just have to see things as they are. It's all obvious. It's all so fucking obvious.' Rachel said: 'For a man, *wife* rhymes with *life*. What rhymes with *husband*? Nothing. *Dustbin*, perhaps.' Jean said: 'I don't think you're giving men much of a chance.' Rachel said: 'Now they know how we feel.'

They started going out once a week: the cinema, a meal, conversations in which each began affectionately to parody the other's stance. On the third evening Jean insisted on paying for dinner; later, in the car outside Jean's house, Rachel leaned across and kissed her on the cheek. 'Better get in before your Dad gets mad at you.'

On the fourth evening, at an Indian restaurant when Jean thought the cook had gone mad with tangerine dye, Rachel suggested that Jean come back to her place. Jean laughed; this time the offer came as less of a surprise.

'But what do they do?' she asked flippantly.

'They?'

'They,' she repeated, meaning *lesbians*, but not bringing herself to say it.

'Well . . .' Rachel said firmly; and Jean at once held up her hand. 'No, I don't mean it. No.' Suddenly in her mind *they* had become *we*; the image seemed preposterous and embarrassing. 'Anyway . . .'

'Anyway what? Anyway the Festival of Britain?'

'Anyway I don't think you're a . . . a *lesbian*.' She managed to say it this time, her pause disinfecting the word, making it sound distant and theoretical, barely applicable to Rachel. Her small blonde companion took her by the wrists, and her fierce brown glare forbade Jean to look away.

'I fuck women,' she said, in a slow, determined voice. 'Is that lesbian enough for you?'

'I like you too much for you to be one.'

'Jean, that's one of your least intelligent remarks.'

'I suppose I mean that isn't a lot of it just getting back at men? What your generation calls political. It's about other things; it's not . . . not just about sex.'

'When was sex only just about sex?'

Always, Jean wanted to say; but it was clear that this would be the wrong answer. Perhaps she didn't have enough experience to argue with Rachel. Why did she always make people cross? Here was Rachel, almost daring her to say something silly. She didn't dare. Or rather, she dared in another direction.

'Anyway, you see, I don't want to.'

'Ah. Well, that's a different argument altogether.'

Jean looked at Rachel, at her jutting chin and fierce brown eyes. How could anyone look so cross; and not cross with disappointment, but cross with desire? All sorts of phrases surfaced in Jean's mind — *she's quite a pretty thing*; *so full of character*; *I'm really rather fond of her* — but they were, she realized, the clichés with which age defuses youth. She felt sorry for Rachel, still young enough for things to turn out right or wrong; the pride or the guilt still lay ahead. And then, beyond that pride or guilt, an age which Jean almost feared to hope for: an age of detachment, a state as much visceral as cerebral. Nowadays, when she heard a story or watched a film, she cared much less whether the ending was happy or unhappy; she just wanted it to turn out properly, correctly, in accordance with its own logic. It was like this with the film of your life. Her ambitions were no longer specifically for happiness or financial security or freedom from disease (though they included all three), but for something more general: the continuing certainty of things. She needed to know that she would carry on being herself.

She couldn't explain all this to Rachel, which is why she said, *Anyway, you see, I don't want to* ... But later, lying awake on a warm night, she wasn't even sure she had meant this. She thought of Prosser in the dispersal hut, rattling the pennies in his pocket. She thought of men in blue uniforms passing the salt more politely than usual, and being quiet in corners.

She didn't surprise herself too much when she agreed to sleep with Rachel. The old need praise just as much as the young, she had said; and desire is a form of praise.

'I'm not so nice to look at any more,' she said when they reached Rachel's flat. She thought of her breasts, her upper arms, her stomach. 'Can you lend me a nightdress?'

Rachel laughed that she didn't own one, but fetched something that served. Jean went to the bathroom, cleaned her teeth, washed, climbed into bed and turned out the light. She lay facing away from the middle of the bed. She heard Rachel's steps, then the weight of a body landing close. Thump. Like Uncle Leslie in the sloping meadow behind the dogleg fourteenth. Jean whispered, 'I think you might have to let me off tonight.'

Rachel fitted herself into the angles of Jean's back. Spoons, Jean thought from her childhood. She and Michael had been like a spoon and a knife. Perhaps this was the answer.

'You don't have to do anything you don't want to,' Rachel said. Jean exhaled in a half-murmur. But what if you didn't want to do anything at all? She lay tensely as Rachel stroked her, making sure she didn't give any inadvertent signal which might be read as pleasure. After a while Rachel stopped. They went to sleep.

Twice more they tried, if try was the word: Jean lay turned away on her side, wearing a borrowed nightdress, holding her breath. She wanted to want to — but the actual achievement of wanting seemed inaccessible. When it seemed that Rachel was asleep, Jean relaxed; she was also struck by how well she then slept. She wondered if they could possibly go on like this. It seemed unlikely. But the idea of anything more brought on thoughts of panic, dryness, age.

'I don't suppose I have the courage to go to bed with you properly, dear,' she said the next time they met.

'It's not brave to go to bed with people. It's usually the opposite.'

'It seems very brave to me. Far too brave. You'll have to let me off.'

'We haven't really tried much, you know.'

'I like the sleeping part,' said Jean, instantly regretting the remark. Rachel was frowning. Why did sex always make people cross? Then a worrying thought came to her.

'You remember that story you told me . . . about not enjoying yourself with someone . . . a man, in bed?'

'Yes.'

'Was that Gregory?'

Rachel laughed. 'No, of course not. If it was I wouldn't have told you.' Jean felt relieved: at least there wasn't some terrible sexual curse running through her family, which was inevitably visited upon Rachel. Later, though, she began to fret: if Rachel could manage a difficult lie with her body, she could surely manage an easy one with her tongue.

Perhaps, despite what Rachel said, it was brave to go to bed with people. Or at least it could be brave. And perhaps she'd run out of her stock of courage. Like Sun-Up Prosser: windy; got the wind-up; yellow; burnt twice. Rachel said it had been brave to leave Michael and brave to bring up Gregory on her own. Jean hadn't seen these actions as brave, merely obvious. Perhaps bravery was a matter of doing the obvious when other people saw it as unobvious. Like Rachel and going to bed. It seemed obvious, and therefore not at all brave, to Rachel; to Jean, unobvious, and it drained her of all courage. People just get used up, Jean thought; their batteries can't be recharged, and nothing can be done about it. Oh dear.

Or perhaps it wasn't really anything to do with courage. Perhaps there should be a different word in peacetime. You shouldn't be allowed to use the word *brave* unless you were a fireman or a bomb-disposal officer or something. You just did things, or you didn't do things, that was all.

* * * *

The news that Uncle Leslie was ill came in a shouted telephone call from his landlady, Mrs Brooks. Since Leslie's return from America, late enough after the war's end for almost nobody to notice, he had sustained himself by a variety of undisclosed jobs, a little gambling, and some astute sponging. He always lived in digs, sometimes moving on rather hurriedly, but in general behaving well. As he grew older his system of barter became more highly developed. 'You wouldn't mind changing this plug for me, would you, Mr Newby?' 'You wouldn't mind letting me share your spot of lunch, would you, Mrs Ferris?' That was the first conversation Gregory could remember his great-uncle taking part in. Several times in recent years Leslie had taken Gregory to the pub, but on no occasion had Gregory seen money change hands, except when it was his round. Perhaps as closing time approached Leslie turned into one of those tame soaks who trundle round the bar collecting glasses in exchange for an evening's drinks, and who echo in a vowel-stretching parody the publican's cry of 'Time, gentlemen, please!'

'Hello, little Jeanie.' It had been years since he had called her that. She was over sixty, but she didn't mind at all.

'How are you?'

'I'm going under, that's how I am. I'm going under.'

'Is that what the doctors say?'

'They don't say because I don't ask.' Uncle Leslie looked thin and yellow, his moustache was ragged, and his thinning black hair held together by a whirlpool of Brylcreem. 'So I've got that thing we don't talk about. I've got a dose of if-he-doesn't-ask-we-won't-tell-him.'

Jean sat on his bed and took his cold, brittle hand. 'You've always been such a brave person,' she said. 'I don't think I'd have set foot outside the country if I hadn't thought of you doing it first. And you sent me to the Pyramids.'

'Well, I don't advise you to follow me where I'm off to now.' Jean was silent. There wasn't much to say. 'Anyway, I was always a bit windy. You probably thought I was quite a dashing fellow, when you were a little girl. I was just as windy then as I am now. Always running away. Always running. I was never brave.'

'There's no bravery without fear,' said Jean rather forcefully. She didn't want Uncle Leslie falling into self-pity. Besides, that was the truth.

'Maybe not,' said Uncle Leslie. His eyes were closed now; he gave a faint yellow smile. 'But I can tell you this. You can have the fear without getting the bravery.'

Jean didn't know what to say, until she remembered a little rustic shelter like an overgrown bird-box.

'Leslie, when we used to go down the Old Green Heaven . . .'

'Ah, do you think that's where old golfers go when they die?' Again, she didn't know what to say. 'No, it's all right, little Jeanie. Old golfers never die, they only lose their balls.'

'When we went down the Old Green Heaven, you used to do your cigarette trick.'

'Which one was that?'

'You used to smoke a whole cigarette without any of the ash dropping off. You used to bend your head back slowly until all the ash balanced on top of itself.'

'Did I do that?' Leslie smiled. At least he had some knowledge, some secrets left. Mostly, the only thing people wanted to find out from those in his position was what it was like to die. 'And you want to know the trick?'

'Yes please.'

'The trick is, you put a needle down the middle of the fag. All that business with bending your head back is just to make it look more real. Same reason you don't do it in a breeze, or outdoors if you can help it, and you get everyone to hold their breath. Make them feel they could wreck it if they don't behave. Always helps, that. You could probably smoke it pointing downwards in a gale and the ash wouldn't drop off. Not that I've tried. But it's hardly the best fag you'll smoke. You keep thinking it tastes of metal.'

'Leslie, you are a clever old thing.'

'Well, you've got to keep something up your sleeve, haven't you?'

On Jean's second visit Leslie looked weaker, and he asked to see Gregory. Since the age of five — when Leslie officially began to acknowledge his existence — his great-nephew had been the recipient of a riddling series of Christmas presents. When six he had been sent a fretwork pipe rack; at seven, a set of stereoscopic viewing cards without the viewer; at ten, the Lysander kit with the missing undercarriage; at eleven, a bicycle pump; at twelve, three linen handkerchiefs with the initial H. Only one letter out, he had thought. When he was fourteen he was sent some French currency which was twenty years out of date and which got him treated as an incompetent fraudster when he tried to change it at the bank; and when he was twenty-one, he received a signed photo of Uncle Leslie, taken many years before, possibly in America. After some early disappointment, Gregory had begun to be secretly proud of his presents; to him they didn't indicate casualness on the part of the giver, but the opposite: a determination to bestow on his great-nephew something entirely characteristic of Uncle Leslie. In this they never failed. Gregory even went for several years in quiet fear that the stereoscopic viewer might turn up, or that his mother might give him one. That would have ruined everything.

Mrs Brooks, with whom Leslie had lodged for almost five years, was a thin, vague woman who for no accountable reason always shouted. It was nothing to do with deafness, as Uncle Leslie had once proved by secretly turning on her radio very softly and watching her reaction; simply a habit which had remained uncorrected for so long that nobody knew its origin, or much cared.

'HE'S VERY POORLY,' she bellowed into the road as she opened the door to Gregory. 'I CAN'T SEE HIM GETTING ANY BETTER,' she roared to the ground and first floors of her establishment as she wrestled Gregory's coat from him. Fortunately, Uncle Leslie's room was on the top floor: a large attic whose tendency to overheat in summer and whose proximity to the gurgling water tanks gave him more than enough leverage when it came to the occasional negotiations about the putative rent.

With shooing motions Gregory had kept Mrs Brooks down on the ground floor. Now he knocked quietly on the attic door and went in. He'd never visited Leslie in his digs before, and on entering immediately felt a strange nostalgia: of course, he thought, this is where all my Christmas presents came from. The place resembled a low-turnover charity-shop: there was a rack of clothes manifestly not intended for the same person; three Hoovers, with spares for a fourth; a cut-glass flower vase with a yellowish scum mark half-way up; a scatter of paperbacks with the top right-hand corner cut off and prices in shillings and pence; a very early Electrolux shaver, nacreous pink in its box, and so old-fashioned in design that it looked like something else, perhaps a sexual appliance of unpopular function; a stack of unmatching dinner plates; several suitcases whose combined capacity far exceeded the contents of the room; and a standard lamp which was switched on even at eleven o'clock on a spring morning.

'Dear Boy,' murmured Leslie, somehow capitalizing the 'Boy' and making Gregory feel it was a term awarded only to the most grown-up people. 'Dear Boy.'

Gregory ignored the plaited-rope linen box with the stoved-in top which appeared to serve as a chair, and sat on his uncle's bed. He didn't know what to say on these occasions — he assumed it must be one of 'these occasions'; but it didn't matter, since Leslie, even when silent for minutes at a time, was always somehow in charge. Mrs Brooks was on his mind.

'Did she tell you how I made her let me die here?'

Gregory knew better than to come-come his uncle. 'No.'

'Told her I'd blab to the Income Tax if she didn't let me.'

'Leslie, you old villain.' Gregory felt it was the kindest compliment he could pay; Leslie took it as intended, and laid a finger along the side of his nose. He seemed too weak to be able to tap it.

'Silly old thing even had to pretend she was my long-lost sister-in-law or something. Only way the hospital would release me. "That's right," I said to her, "you claim the body." They didn't like that at the hospital. Have a pill, meboy.' He gestured towards the line of plastic cylinders by his bedside. Gregory shook his head. 'Can't say I blame you, lad. Don't care for them myself.'

They sat in silence for a while, Leslie with his eyes closed. His hair was as black as it had ever been — perhaps he had some cut-price potion in his sponge-bag, Gregory thought — but his eyebrows were pure white and his moustache half-and-half. His skin had yellowed and fallen away from the bones of his face; yet even in repose there was something about his expression that could charm. He looked like the sort of fairground barker who invites you in to see the Bearded Lady. You go in, and you know the lady's beard is simply glued on, and he knows that you know, and you know that he knows that you know, but it is somehow impossible to hold this against him. 'Don't miss the Bearded Lady,' you find yourself announcing as you stumble out past the hesitating crowd. 'Finest Bearded Lady south of Hadrian's Wall.'

Occasionally, Leslie would say something, his eyes trying to open as his mouth did. He didn't mention his death again, and Gregory assumed the matter was now closed. He talked a little of Jean, at one point confiding to Gregory, 'She used to be a real screamer, your mum,' before closing his eyes again.

Gregory wondered what he meant. Perhaps 'screamer' was someone who was 'fast', as they used to call it. But that hardly seemed right for his mother. It must be some piece of pre-war slang. He'd look it up if he remembered.

After a while he wanted to tell Leslie how fond he had always been of him, and how much he had enjoyed those wartime yarns Jean disapproved of. But this seemed tactless, somehow, almost cruel. Instead, he murmured, 'Do you remember those stereoscopic cards you gave me? I was thinking about them only the other day.'

'The what?'

'Those cards. Sort of colour transparencies, only two of them side by side. Then you put them in a viewer and held it up to the light and saw pictures of African game parks or the Grand Canyon. Only . . . only you never gave me the viewer.' Try as he might, Gregory couldn't keep a note of complaint out of his voice, even though he felt no such emotion inside.

'Huh,' said Leslie, his eyes firmly shut. 'Huh.' Was he reflecting on his own meanness or his nephew's ingratitude? Slowly, the eyes opened, and directed themselves past Gregory's shoulder. 'If you look over there you'll probably find the other bit.'

'No. No, Uncle, really. I . . . I don't really want the other bit.'

One eye stayed open briefly, surveyed him, judged him too daft for words, and closed itself. A couple of minutes later, Leslie said, 'Take the shaver instead.'

'What?'

'I said take the shaver instead.' Gregory looked across to the top of the chest of drawers. The Electrolux gleamed pinkly at him.

'Thanks very much.' It was, he realized, the perfect present.

'Because if you don't she'll only take it to do her legs with.'

Gregory chuckled, and a faint smile tweaked his lips. He gazed at his uncle's fairground face. Finally, without opening his eyes, Leslie pronounced the last words Gregory heard him say.

'This isn't about the Common Market, you know.'

Indeed not. Gregory rose, placed his hand flat against his uncle's shoulder, gave him the softest shake that was possible, collected the shaver from the chest of drawers, hid it in a pocket in case Mrs Brooks thought he had stolen it (which is precisely what she did think when she discovered it was missing), and left.

After Leslie's death, Gregory helped Mrs Brooks clean out the attic.

'BETTER SEND IT ALL TO OXFAM,' she shouted, just to alert the second and third floors of her establishment. When they moved the bed, Gregory trod on something that crunched sharply. It was a small bag of fish and chips, thrown there months before and long desiccated of their oil. Gregory picked it up and looked around for the waste-paper basket. There wasn't one. All this junk, he thought, and nowhere to throw it.

At his office, while he bargained with those who sought money in exchange for their demise, Gregory thought back over Uncle Leslie's life and death. He had been not just touched, but impressed by Leslie's behaviour on that last visit. He had mentioned his impending death as soon as Gregory arrived, had wrapped it up in a joke, and then talked about other things. He hadn't made it into a farewell, though that was certainly what it was; he hadn't given way to self-pity, or encouraged tears in his visitor. All of which made Leslie's death less upsetting than it might have been. Gregory supposed that Leslie had been, for want of a better word, brave.

It seemed to make a point, this death. Leslie, who had run away from the war, who had fiddled and scrounged, who might have been called a spiv even by Jean if he hadn't been a member of the family, had died with courage, even grace. Or was that too neat, too much of a morality? After all, they weren't certain Leslie had actually run away from the war — that was only what Jean's father said; Leslie himself referred to the time as 'when I was Stateside'. They didn't know either that his bartering system of life wasn't forced on him by penury; and Gregory didn't really know how Leslie had died, how the end had been. Perhaps the pills took away all his pain; in which case, could you be said to be brave? Well, yes, in that you had to face the knowledge of your own death. But perhaps they had pills to take away that knowledge, to purge and sweeten it. Gregory expected that they did.

So what was a good death? Was it possible to have a good death any more; or was it in any case an illusion to believe that there had been good deaths — brave, stoical, consoling, affectionate deaths — in the past? Was 'a good death' one of those phrases which didn't, in fact, have anything to which it referred; was it like naming an animal that didn't exist — a winged crocodile, say? Or perhaps a good death was simply this: the best death you could manage in the circumstances, regardless of medical help. Or again, more simply still: a good death was any death not swamped by agony, fear and protest. By that count — indeed, by almost any count — Uncle Leslie had had a good death.

*　　*　　*　　*

Jean remembered China. Perhaps this was why she hadn't felt as much of a stranger there as she had expected: because being in China was like living with a man. Men juggled with goldfish and expected you to be impressed. Men gave you fur coats made out of dogs. Men invented the plastic bonsai. Men gave you very small address books which they thought would meet your needs. Men were in places very primitive: they rode to market with pigs roped across the back wheels of their bicycles. Most of all there was the way men talked to you. In Asian times. The temple was repented. We grow ladies. Here is the sobbing centre. They talked at you through a megaphone even though you stood only a couple of yards away. And when the batteries failed, they still preferred to shout down the instrument at you rather than adopt the frail equality of the voice. Or else they talked at you from the other side of a curving wall, and as you craned your neck you could barely detach their voice from dozens of others. And when you asked them the simplest questions — 'Do you want to go to Shanghai?' — they would not answer. They pretended there was something wrong with the question. That is not a real question. Why do you ask such a thing? There is no answer because there is no question. Here is the sobbing centre. Put your finger on the knot and help me rope the pig. The temple was repented. In Asian times. Do not forget we live in Asian times; we have always lived in Asian times.

THREE

Immortality is no learned question.

Kierkegaard

How do you tell a good life from a bad life, a wasted life? Jean remembered the forewoman at the jade factory in China who was asked how you could tell good jade from bad jade. Through an interpreter, and through a megaphone that didn't work, came the reply, 'You look at it and by looking you tell its qualities.' Nowadays, this answer no longer seemed so evasive.

Jean had often wondered what it would be like to grow old. When she had been in her fifties, and still feeling in her thirties, she heard a talk on the radio by a gerontologist. 'Put cotton wool in your ears,' he had said, 'and pebbles in your shoes. Pull on rubber gloves. Smear Vaseline over your glasses, and there you have it: instant ageing.'

It was a good test, but it naturally contained a flaw. You never did age instantly; you never did have a sharp memory for comparison. Nor, when she looked back over the last forty of her hundred years, did it seem to be initially, or even mainly, a matter of sensory deprivation. You grew old first not in your own eyes, but in other people's eyes; then, slowly, you agreed with their opinion of you. It wasn't that you couldn't walk as far as you used to, it was that other people didn't expect you to; and if they didn't, then it needed vain obstinacy to persist.

At sixty she had still felt like a young woman; at eighty, she felt like a middle-aged woman who had something a bit wrong with her; at nearly a hundred she no longer bothered to think whether or not she felt younger than she was — there didn't seem any point. She was relieved not to be bedbound, as she might have been in earlier times; but mostly she took the medical advances of her lifetime for granted. She lived increasingly inside her head, and was content to be there. Memories, there were far too many memories; they raced across her sky like Irish weather. Her feet, with each succeeding year, seemed a little farther away from her hands; she dropped things, stumbled a little, was fearful; but mostly what she noticed was the smirking paradox of old age: how everything seemed to take longer than it used to, but how, despite this, time seemed to go faster.

At eighty-seven, Jean had taken up smoking. Cigarettes had been finally pronounced risk-free, and after dinner she would light one, close her eyes, and suck on some tangy memory from the previous century. Her favourite brand was Numbers, a cigarette which when first introduced had been divided by dotted lines into eighteen mean smoking units. These MSUs were numbered one to eighteen — a benevolent ploy by the manufacturer which was designed to help people know how much of their cigarette they had smoked. After a couple of years, though, in a summer when subjects for computer-lobby had been hard to find, a row took place (one which, in the manufacturers' eyes, got way out of hand) over whether it was paternalistic and oppressive to number Numbers. Finally, after an 8 per cent nationwide canvas and a few unpleasant incidents (the marketing director's car had been painted with dotted lines and divided into eighteen sections from bonnet to boot), the manufacturers agreed to produce unnumbered Numbers.

Even so, Jean still automatically thought of her cigarette as containing eighteen puffs. Six, six and six; she would lay it down between each of the three sections. The first six puffs inflated her with sudden pleasure; they were a new burst of life. The second six were less active, striving to keep her on the plateau she had naively attained without difficulty; the final six contained a streak of panic: she would watch the fire burn closer to her fingers, and sometimes try to turn six into seven. But this never made any difference.

Jean also enjoyed sitting in the sun. Perhaps, she thought, this was something to do with your skin: as it grew leathery, spotted and reptilian, so it made you start behaving like a lizard. Sometimes she would put on an old pair of white gloves rather than look at her hands.

'Is your skin itching?' Gregory would ask.

'Just keeping my herb sausages out of sight.'

Gregory, nearing sixty, still had the round, gentle face Jean remembered from their travelling days together, and occasionally a sudden, intense look in his eye would recall to her the things he had gazed at in his life: his rainbow battlefleet of aeroplanes, his computer chess-set, his pallid girlfriends. But now only memory could make him young. She had become, she realized, the mother of an old man. His hair was quite grey, his round gold glasses looked like antiques, and his careful, quizzical manner increasingly had an air of elderly pedantry about it. Gregory went to work twice a week; he played with GPC; he sat in his room listening to jazz. Sometimes she felt that a morning mist lay over his life and had never properly risen.

Jean no longer cared to examine herself in the mirror. Not from vanity, but lack of interest. You could be intrigued or alarmed by only so many elastications of the flesh; another one was scarcely news. She wore her hair in a loose bun; she had not washed it for several years, and its whiteness had now moved into an accumulated yellowness. How strange, she thought: as a child I was approximately blonde; now, in second childhood, I am allowed a second, false yellowness. She had shrunk an inch or two from her mature height; she stooped a little, and held on to furniture as she moved about the house. She had long since given up following public events; her character seemed less important to her than it once had; her eyes had lost some of their blue and taken on the milky grey of a morning sky that has yet to make up its mind. It was as if the oxygen supply had a small leak in it: things were becoming slower, and more general. The difference was that she knew it, and so could not share the ignorant joy of those long-dead fliers who parodied old age as they strained towards the sun.

Occasionally, Gregory would try introducing her to other very old people, and be disappointed by her lack of enthusiasm. 'But I've never been very interested in old people,' she would explain. 'Why should I start now?'

'But couldn't you . . . I don't know . . . talk about old times?'

'Gregory,' she replied with a certainty that sounded like severity, '*I'm* not interested in *their* old times, and as for mine, I'm keeping them to myself. You can be interested in old people when you're old yourself.'

Gregory smiled. Old age? He didn't even have a life insurance policy. The firm had offered him a special rate, of course, but he declined. People said that an insurance salesman without a policy was like a vegetarian butcher. The joke didn't deter him. He would nod, and think to himself that there was logic in being a vegetarian butcher: if you spent your day cutting up animals, you might well not want to go home and eat them for dinner. Even if you got a cut rate on your cut meat.

He was well into his fifties when he began to brood about suicide. It was a quiet, almost companionable brooding; not a melodrama with lightning across a carbon-paper sky, but a discreet, determined line of thought. Perhaps it had something to do with not having an insurance policy, whose terms would forbid melancholy action, and presumably discourage melancholy speculation as well. Or perhaps it was just that suicide had been much in the news during the first decade of the century. It was said that some people fell in love only because they heard love being talked about; the same might be true of suicide.

All those old people killing themselves. Gregory could still remember some of the names: Freddy Page, David Salisbury, Sheila Abley. Plus the name everyone knew: Don Johnson. Predictably, the newspapers and television had misunderstood the first few Old People's Suicides. Editorialists pointed out that euthanasia had been legal for eight years, that the state provided the best soft-termination facilities in Europe; why should these people kill themselves in such a noisy and public fashion unless they were seriously disturbed? In which case we must increase the Geriatric Monitoring Service in their areas, and see that soft-term leaflets are more widely available.

But the campaign only became more efficient. There was an Old People's Martyr on the first of every month from March to September 2006; the OPS coordinating committee announced its existence; while the papers discovered that news about old people, if treated in a dramatic enough way, did not necessarily decrease circulation. When the OPS committee's telephone was tapped, even this redounded to its favour: the view was openly expressed that it was wrong to bug old people's phones.

On October 1 Mervyn Danbury, the popular cricket commentator, shot himself in St Paul's Cathedral Museum holding a birthday card signed by the Prime Minister. Shortly afterwards the OPS committee produced its first list of demands, assembled — or so it was claimed — after an unpublicised computer phone-in polling 37 per cent of the over-seventies. The demands were as follows. 1) Stop all advertising of soft-termination facilities. 2) Close down all old people's homes. 3) Eliminate the word geriatric and its cognates from official use. 4) Old people are to be known in future as old people. 5) Old people are to be loved more. 6) There shall be a special series of awards to recognize wisdom, and the achievements of old people. 7) Creation of an Old People's Day, to be celebrated once a year. 8) Positive discrimination in jobs and housing in favour of old people. 9) Free fundrugs for the over-eighties.

At first the government said it refused to negotiate under duress; but then Don Johnson burnt himself to death between the sentry-boxes outside Buckingham Palace. Pictures of the blackened wheelchair and its sad sack of collapsed flesh were on the front page of every newspaper. The government's slur campaign, which sought to establish Johnson as an unstable and dislikable character who had quite possibly been murdered in a grudge killing, misfired. Most of the committee's demands were conceded within weeks; as a sign of repentance for its earlier scepticism, the government even suggested that Old People's Day be named Don Johnson Day. Television helped make old people not just acceptable, but fashionable; there was a spate of marriages between very old and very young partners; stamps bearing the portraits of Famous Old People were issued; the Old People's Games were instituted; and Gregory invited his mother to live in a small, sunny room at the back of his house.

There were the usual jokes made: he's hoping you'll become a videostar and put him on your show; he's only after your fundrugs; and so on. Occasionally, she worried about Gregory's motives; but as soon as she asked herself whether people should be bullied into goodness, she would snappily reply that of course they should, because that was the only way most of them were going to get there. In fact, she and Gregory never discussed his motives for asking her; nor hers for accepting.

* * * *

The General Purposes Computer was begun in 1998 after a series of government inquiries. Previously, in the late Eighties, there had been various pilot schemes which had sought to put the whole of human knowledge on to an easily accessible record. The Funlearn Project of 1991–2, with officially sponsored prizes and scholarships, had been the best known of these schemes; but its purity of principle had been impugned when it was linked to a government campaign to decrease the child-user percentage in state videogame parlours. Some had even accused Funlearn of didacticism.

Inevitably the early schemes had been book-oriented; they were attempts to create the ultimate, perfect library where 'readers' (as they were still archaically known) could obtain access to the world's accumulation of knowledge. Objections were raised, however, that these schemes were all too scholar-biased: those accustomed to use books would now be able to use them more efficiently, whereas those who were not would be further disadvantaged. Three government reports in the mid-1990s all suggested that a more democratic user-base was required before one of these pilot schemes could qualify for full state backing.

GPC was thus constructed to be information-centred; the enquirer called up not book titles but subject categories. Sources, while relevant at the input stage in assessing the reliability of the facts, were held to be irrelevant at the output stage, and were therefore suppressed. Scholars claimed that such an absence of supportive bibliography invalidated the whole of the GPC programme; but democrats dismissed them as melodramatic, and argued that this suppression would draw off the conceit of writers — or source-providers, as they became known. Rendering information anonymous was like milking the venom from a snake, they said. Only now would knowledge become truly democratic.

GPC, finally opened in 2003, stored everything hitherto contained in all books published in all languages; researchers had emptied radio and TV archives, book, record and tape libraries, newspapers, magazines, folk memory. ALL THINGS KNOWN TO PEOPLE ran the slogan carved on a stone videoscreen above the entrances to municipal GPCHQs. Scholars complained of defective input in several areas, and that the concept of 'Total Knowledge' was at odds with what they referred to as 'Correct Knowledge'; cynics observed that the only things, you couldn't ask GPC about were its own input, sources, principles and personnel; but democrats were happy, and when asked to join the debate about total versus correct knowledge referred to angels dancing on a pinhead. Of course, GPC might be used for settling bets and calling up football results; but there was no harm in that. More important, it permitted the setting-up of a new range of personalized and flexitimed evening classes. Above all, democrats felt comforted by the symbol of GPC, by the idea of a final repository of information, an oracle of fact.

Not only was GPC democratic in input, it was also democratic in output. You keyed in with your social security number, and output was modified to your level of understanding. This initially contentious aspect of GPC was quickly accepted as necessary. It was said that GPC analysed your questions as you tapped them in and made its own continuous assessment of your understanding, which it then used, if necessary, to update your social security listing; but this had never been confirmed. People, especially democrats, soon learned to rely on GPC; they became fond of it. Some became more than fond, and there were cases of GPC-addiction being cited in the divorce courts.

Gradually, legend began to grow like ivy round this silo of facts. It was said that, as well as the democratic output modifier, there was also a facility enabling secret operators to break in to the circuit and alter responses. It was said that the way to get the best answers out of GPC was to lie with your questions. It was said that there was a hook-up between GPC and New Scotland Yard III, and that posers of dubious questions (where is the most valuable collection of silver belonging to an absentee owner?) had been picked up as they left the building.

Most of the legends, however, surrounded a function of GPC called TAT. It had been added as an information category in 2008, after a brief period of intense and mysteriously funded lobbying. TAT stood for The Absolute Truth. In the old days of book-libraries, there had been private cases for works (obscene, blasphemous or politically contentious) which could be examined only on personal application; now GPC had an information category which could be keyed into only with special permission. Cynics made a historical comparison and claimed that Truth was now proved to be a blasphemous obscenity subject to political manipulation; but democrats affirmed the citizen's inalienable right of access to the most serious speculations and conclusions currently available.

Since TAT was a late addition to GPC, its presence was not acknowledged in the official manifest. Some people didn't even believe that the function existed. Others believed it did, but weren't too interested. Most people knew somebody who knew somebody who had applied, or had thought of applying, for TAT; but nobody seemed to know anyone who had actually done so. Cynics maintained that you had to bring a doctor's certificate, a will, and a permission slip signed by three members of your family; democrats replied that standard will forms and autowitnessing were naturally available in the TAT foyer, but that you shouldn't jump to conclusions.

It was confidently and variously asserted that several TAT-enquirers had gone mad; that there was a pharmaceutical dispenser attached to the console and questioners were supplied not just with facts and opinions but also with fundrugs, slumberpills and even soft-termination tablets; that people in perfect health had gone down to GPC determined to ask for TAT and never been seen again.

Nobody was even quite sure what it was that TAT knew or did. Some thought it gave you lifechoices, like a sophisticated careers guidance officer; others that it specialized in existential decisions; others again that in some way it allowed you to practise the pure exercise of free will: it was like those simulation cockpits in which they trained airline pilots. You could learn to take off and land; or, if you preferred, to crash. A rumour began that funding for the TAT lobby had come from the same source as funding for the Soft Termination Lobby back in the Nineties; but nobody could be sure. Most people liked to know that TAT was there, should they ever need it; but few were inclined to try. It seemed like having a long-stop at cricket: more for the wicket-keeper's peace of mind than for any regular use.

'Spoken like TAT' became a proverbial phrase for a while; though curiously no one quite knew how TAT spoke. Everyone agreed that its answers must be differently phrased from the rest of GPC's output; they were believed to be clear, yet poetically expressed. Some people said that writers had been recruited to create a special TAT tongue, both resonant and ambiguous. Some people said that TAT spoke in verse; others that it spoke in baby language.

'When I was a child,' Jean said to Gregory after she had finished her evening cigarette, 'I used to ask myself questions in bed. I suppose it was instead of praying: I wasn't encouraged to pray. I don't know how long I did it for; it feels like my whole childhood, but I expect it was only a year or two.'

'Like what?'

'Oh, I can't remember them all. I remember wanting to know whether there was a sandwich museum, and if so where it was. And why Jews didn't like golf. And how Mussolini knew which way the paper folded. And whether heaven was up the chimney. And why the mink is excessively tenacious of life.'

'And did you get any answers?'

'I'm not sure. I can't remember whether I actually got the answers or stopped being interested in the questions. I suppose that as I grew up I realized that the museum I'd imagined to contain Queen Victoria's egg-and-cress sandwich was a fairly silly idea, and I found out that Jews did like golf it was just that golfers didn't like Jews, and as for heaven being up the chimney, I suppose I learned that certain questions have to be rephrased before you can get an answer to them.' She paused, and looked across at Gregory. 'And I never did find out why the mink is excessively tenacious of life. It used to worry me a lot. I used to think, perhaps that's why mink coats are so highly prized — because the fur comes from an animal which has given up its life with extreme reluctance. Like minerals being valuable because they are difficult to extract. Do you remember mink farms?'

Gregory frowned. He couldn't remember. So many things had gone on in the time before wildlife had been returned to the wild.

'I always wondered about mink farms. How they killed them, I mean. They wouldn't want to damage the fur, after all. They'd hardly want to try strangling them. Perhaps they gassed them, like badgers.'

Gregory didn't know. He couldn't even remember about gassing badgers. How barbarous the past had been. No terminations had been soft; not even for badgers.

The next day, at GPC, he called up the NATHIST bank.

'Mink,' he typed in.

READY.

'Why is the mink excessively tenacious of life?'

There was a pause, a green flash of WAIT, and after a few seconds the reply: NOT REAL QUESTION.

Come off it, thought Gregory. That's too easy. Sometimes this silo of knowledge could be very curmudgeonly with its grain. Still, you could occasionally trick it by simply repeating the question.

'Why is the mink excessively tenacious of life?'

NOT REAL QUESTION.

Ah well, back to basics instead.

'Is it difficult to kill a mink?'

FERAL SLAUGHTER PROHIBITED STATUTE . . .

Gregory keyed in an Interrupt. Start again.

'When were mink farms prohibited?'

1998.

'Request information running mink farms.' He waited ten seconds or so.

READY.

'How did workers on mink farms kill the mink?'

VARIOUS. SPECIFICALLY POISONS, GASSING, SOMETIMES MECHANI-CAL, ALSO ELECTROCUTION.

Gregory shivered. The brutal old days.

'Did the mink take a long time to die?'

ELECTROCUTION 2·3 SECONDS . . .

Interrupt.

'Does the mink struggle hard against death?'

YES. WANT EXAMPLES?

Gregory didn't want examples. That was one of the troubles with GPC: it was so full of information it always tried to give you as much of it as possible; like some party bore, it wanted to drag you away from your own interests and boast of its knowledge instead.

'Why?'

WHY WHAT? EXPAND.

'Why does the mink struggle hard against death?'

NOT REAL QUESTION.

Bastard, thought Gregory. Bastard. But he continued, as tenacious as the mink itself.

'Why does the mink struggle harder against death than other animals?'

ARGUFY. SUGGEST C37.

Gregory keyed in C37 without much expectation. ARGUFY indicated that the information sought by input was still in dispute among the world's experts. C37 gave him an abbreviated rundown on the current state of evolutionary theory. All that it told him, though, was that the mink's instinctive struggle against death was one reason why it had survived so long and so well as a species. Which really didn't get him any further.

He decided not to tell Jean about the various ways in which mink were killed. It wasn't that it would upset her; he just didn't want to go through it again himself.

'I asked GPC why the mink is excessively tenacious of life.'

'Did you, dear? That's very thoughtful of you.'

'Well, I thought you wanted to know.'

'And what did it say, this clever–clogs machine of yours?' Jean awaited the answer with some scepticism; she didn't believe in computer knowledge. She was, she admitted, hopelessly old-fashioned.

'It said that it wasn't a real question.'

Jean laughed. In a way, she was quite pleased.

'About ninety years ago,' she said, 'though it might have been a bit longer come to think of it, I asked my father the time. He told me three o'clock. I asked him why it was three o'clock, and he said exactly the same thing. He took his pipe out of his mouth, pointed the stem at me, and said, "Jean, that's not a real question."'

But what were real questions, she wondered. Real questions were limited to those questions to which the people you asked already knew the answers. If her father or GPC could answer, that made the enquiry a real question; if not, it was dismissed as being falsely based. How very unfair. Because it was these questions, the ones that weren't real, to which you wanted to know the answers most pressingly. For ninety years she'd wanted to know about the mink. Her father had failed, so had Michael; and now GPC was ducking it. That was the way it was. Knowledge didn't really advance, it only seemed to. The serious questions always remained unanswered.

'While you're at it, dear, could you find out what happens to the skin after death?'

'Really, Mother.'

'No, I mean it.' Jean increasingly found herself remembering times she thought she had forgotten: distant years now proved easier to recall than more recent ones. This was, of course, normal; but it had its sudden pleasures. Gregory bent over his aeroplanes: she could see him now. He would cover the balsa skeleton with tissue-paper. The tissue-paper would be sprinkled with water and pull tight as it dried. Then he would paint it with dope, and again it would sag and pucker. Then, gradually, as it dried once more, it became tougher and tauter still.

Perhaps this happened to the skin as well. It seemed fairly tight at first, then as you got older it sagged and puckered as if you'd been sprinkled with water and painted with dope. Perhaps, after death, it dried out and stretched tightly over your bones. Perhaps you looked your best, all smart and finished, only after your death.

'Go on Gregory.'

'No, I won't. It's morbid.'

'Of course it is.' She bet she was right. When they exhumed those people who'd been buried in bogs, wasn't their skin all dry and tight, the wrinkles eased out, as if death really had smoothed the cares away? 'Well, perhaps you can find out what happened to Lindbergh's sandwiches instead.'

'Sandwiches?'

'Yes. Lindbergh. He was probably before your time. He flew the Atlantic all by himself. He took five sandwiches with him and only ate one and a half. All my life I've wanted to know what happened to the rest.'

'I'll see if GPC can help.' Really, there were times . . .

'I shouldn't think it can. I haven't much of an opinion of that mincing machine of yours.'

'You haven't even been near it, Mother.'

'No, but I can imagine. There used to be something like it when I was a girl. He was called the Memory Man. He used to go round fairs and things. You could ask him any old rubbish — football scores or something — and he could tell you without any trouble. Ask him anything useful and he was no help at all.'

'Did you ever ask him anything?'

'No, but I can imagine.'

* * * *

How do people die? Gregory called up the last words of the famous. Kings seemed to die in one of two ways: either crying 'Villain, villain' as the murderer's knife struck, or else adjusting their knee-breeches in the confident expectation of soon entering another court which would be much like their own, if slightly — ever so slightly — grander. Clerics died with a squint: one eye cast down in obedience, the other one raised in hope. Writers died with writerly things on their lips, still wanting to be remembered, still unsure to the very last whether all those words they had written would do the trick. There had been an American poet, a woman, whose final words had been, 'I must go in, the fog is rising.' All very well, thought Gregory, but you had to be sure of your timing. You couldn't very well produce your carefully scripted farewell and then go on living, else your last recorded words might turn out to be 'Get me another hot-water bottle.'

Artists seemed better at it than writers, more matter-of-fact. He admired the French painter's modest wish: 'I hope with all my heart there will be painting in heaven.' Or perhaps it was that foreigners were better at dying than Anglo-Saxons. An Italian painter, urged to receive a priest, had replied, 'No, I am curious to see what happens in the next world to those who die unshriven.' A Swiss physician died feeling his own pulse and announcing to a colleague in attendance, 'My friend, the artery ceases to beat.' Professional deaths like these pleased Gregory. He warmed to the French grammarian who declared, 'Je vas, ou je vais, mourir: l'un ou l'autre se dit.'

Were these good deaths? Was a good death one where the character of the life about the extinguished was maintained until the end? The composer Rameau on his deathbed complained of a curé hitting the wrong note; the painter Watteau rejected a crucifix offered him because the artist's representation of Christ was unworthy. And should a good death somehow imply that life was a little over-rated, and hence that fears about death were exaggerated? Is a good death one that leaves the mourners undistressed? Is a good death one that leaves those present something to think about? Gregory chuckled at the American writer who asked, *in extremis*, 'What is the answer?' and, receiving no reply, continued, 'In that case, what is the question?'

Or perhaps how they died was affected by why they died. Go straight to the top, thought Gregory, and typed in 'Fetch American Presidents'. A list appeared on the screen, with a flashing circle to indicate further material was available if required. The names only went up to Grover Cleveland, but Gregory thought that was probably enough. He typed 'Cause of Death' into the Enquiry Field, and contemplated the twenty-two Presidents in front of him. Some were vaguely familiar; others sounded more like corn-dealers, dry-goods merchants and pharmacists. Corner-shop names redolent of small-town honesty. Franklin Pierce, Millard Fillmore, John Tyler, Rutherford Hayes . . . even Americans didn't seem to be called things like that any more. Gregory suddenly felt nostalgia — not the everyday and sentimental kind that you feel for your own childhood, but the fiercer, purer form set off by an era you could not possibly have known.

Of course, he realized, some of these Iowa seed-drill merchants were probably just as crooked and incompetent as the known criminals who had inhabited the White House. But that seemed no reason for cancelling his request. He moved the blinking green cursor down the list until it rested on the F of Franklin Pierce, then tapped 'Proceed'.

8 OCT 1869 ABDOMINAL DROPSY.

Hmm. He moved the cursor up to Thomas Jefferson.

4 JULY 1826 CHRONIC DIARRHOEA.

Rutherford B. Hayes.

17 JAN 1893 PARALYSIS OF THE HEART.

The diagnoses sounded charmingly distant: frontier euphemisms for causes not properly understood. This part of GPC's bank probably hadn't been updated for years. Gregory approved: it was right that the cause of your death should be given in the language of your own time. It was somehow proper.

Zachary Taylor, CHOLERA MORBUS AFTER PARTAKING IMMODERATELY OF ICED WATER AND ICED MILK THEN LATER A LARGE QUANTITY OF CHERRIES. Ulysses S. Grant, CANCER OF THE TONGUE. That seemed a little closer to home. Gregory clacked his way quietly through the list. Bright's disease. Debility. Shot. Shot. Dropsy. Asthma. Cholera. Rheumatic Gout. Enfeebled health. Old age.

The list gave Gregory a sense of rising envy. How varied and romantic were the ways of death then. Nowadays you died only of soft termination, old age, or from one of the diminishing band of trite diseases. Dropsy ... asthma ... cholera morbus ... it seemed like an extension of freedom to have so many possibilities ahead. Gregory lingered over Rutherford B. Hayes. Paralysis of the heart. You probably experienced just as much pain and fear as with any other ailment; but what a thing to have said about you. He died of Paralysis of the Heart, Gregory whispered to himself. Perhaps Casanova should have died of that too. It made him want to invent at least one new cause of death, something to surprise his own age with. In the 1980s they had discovered a fresh category of illness, he suddenly remembered; it was called Allergy to the Twentieth Century. The victims — few, but well-publicized — experienced chronic reaction to every aspect of modern life. They might have responded in just the same way to the nineteenth century, but their disease would then have been given a firm yet fragrant name like brain fever. The more self-doubting twentieth century preferred to call the illness an allergy to its own times. Gregory wished he could produce some malady as original as that. A final tremor of invention with which to say farewell. He forgot why he had asked for Presidents' deaths. He checked on Casanova: no, not Paralysis of the Heart, just old age.

'I suppose one consolation', Gregory said that evening to his mother, 'is that it can't go on.'

'Oh no. It doesn't go on. It ends. That's the point, isn't it?'

'Ah. No. I meant the thinking about it, rather than the actual going on. GPC came up with a good line when I was asking something else. About how it was impossible to look at either the sun or death without blinking.'

Jean Serjeant smiled, in a way that seemed to her son almost smug. No, perhaps that wasn't right — after all, she never liked appearing clever; perhaps she was just remembering something. Gregory watched her; slowly, she closed her eyes, as if the darkness helped her see more clearly into the past. When her lids were finally shut, she spoke.

'You *can* stare at the sun. Twenty years before you were born I knew someone who learned to stare at the sun.'

'Through a piece of smoked glass?'

'No.' Slowly, and without opening her eyes, she brought her left hand up in front of her face, then eased the fingers apart. 'He was a pilot. He had to learn about the sun. After a while you can get used to it. You just have to look at it through parted fingers; then you can manage. You can stare at the sun for as long as you like.' Perhaps, she thought, perhaps after a while you begin to grow webbing between your fingers.

'That must be quite a trick,' said Gregory. 'Though I suppose it's hard to tell whether you want to learn it or not.'

Jean opened her eyes and looked at her hand. She was surprised, and a little alarmed. She had forgotten how much her knuckles had swollen over the last thirty years. Short pieces of rope threaded with hazelnuts, that's what her fingers looked like now. And her knobbly knuckles meant that when she tried to part her fingers slowly, open the slats gently like Venetian blinds, she immediately let in brash chunks of light. She couldn't do what Sun-Up Prosser had been able to do. She was very old, and her fingers let in far too much light.

'Do you think', said Gregory nervously, 'that there's no point worrying about it all then?'

'It?'

'It. God. Faith. Religion. Death.'

'Heaven.'

'Well ...'

'No, Heaven, that's what you mean. That's all anyone ever means. Get me to Heaven. How much is a ticket to Heaven? It's all so ... feeble-minded. Anyway, I've been to Heaven.'

'?'

'Heaven. I've been to Heaven.'

'What was it like?'

'Very dusty.'

Gregory smiled. His mother's tendency to the enigmatic was definitely increasing. Someone who didn't know her might have thought her mind was wandering; but Gregory knew there was always a sure point of reference, something which in her own terms made sense. Probably it just took too long to explain. Gregory wondered if this was what being old meant: everything you wanted to say required a context. If you gave the full context, people thought you a rambling old fool. If you didn't give the context, people thought you a laconic old fool. The very old needed interpreters just as the very young did. When the old lost their companions, their friends, they also lost their interpreters: they lost love, but they also lost the full power of speech.

Jean was remembering her visit to Heaven. To the Temple of Heaven in Beijing as they called it. At least they hadn't renamed Heaven as well. A dry June morning with the dust blowing straight in from the Gobi desert. A woman was bicycling to work with her baby. The baby's head was swathed in gauze to protect it from the dust. The baby looked like a tiny bee-keeper.

At the Temple of Heaven the dust had swirled in playful circles round the courtyard. She had seen the back of an old Chinaman. A blue cap, a wrinkled neck, a wrinkled tunic. The tortoise neck stretching out sideways to the great curve of the Echo Wall. The Chinaman was listening to a conversation he could not possibly understand. Perhaps the words sounded beautiful to him, the voices transcendental. But Jean had put her ear to the wall and understood: something rude about a dead Chinese leader, then some amatory prattle. Nothing more than that. That was all there was to hear.

Jean knew, of course, what Gregory was doing. He was rattling the pennies in his pocket. He was screaming at the sky. All this panic he thought he was concealing so well from her: it was just a grown-up way of doing what she and Uncle Leslie had done nearly a century ago beyond the smelly beeches at the dogleg fourteenth. Putting your head back and roaring at the empty heavens, knowing that however much noise you made, nobody up there would hear you. And then you flopped down on your back, exhausted, self-conscious and a little pleased: even if no one was listening, you had somehow made your point. That was what Gregory was doing. He was making his point. She just hoped that when he flopped down he wouldn't hurt himself in the fall.

Playfully, Gregory began to quiz GPC about suicide. Cautiously, too: you never knew if there wasn't an automatic operator interrupt when input veered on to certain matters. Who knows, a carton of happy pills might drop into his lap from a secret dispenser, or a holiday-camp voucher might turn up in the next morning's post.

The dangerous charm of GPC was that everything in the world could be called up; if you didn't look out, a couple of sessions might turn you from a serious enquirer into a mere gape-mouthed browser. Gregory found himself swiftly diverted into the arcana of suicide. He dallied, for instance, with the famous copycat suicide of Mr Budgell, who had left a performance of Addison's *Cato* and flung himself into the Thames, leaving behind the following defence of his action:

> What Cato did, and Addison approved,
> Cannot be wrong.

Gregory called up a summary of the play and felt sorry for Mr Budgell. Cato had killed himself as a protest against dictatorship and as a rebuke to his fellow-countrymen. Poor Mr Budgell: nobody had felt in the least rebuked by his departure.

Slightly more convincing was the example of Robeck, the Swedish professor who wrote a long tract exhorting readers to suicide, then put to sea in an open boat to practise what he preached. Gregory tried to discover from GPC how many copies Robeck's work had sold, and how many suicides it had provoked; but there were no statistics available. Instead, he moved on, browsing among Japanese pantheists who loaded their pockets with stones and plunged into the sea before admiring relatives; transported slaves from West Africa, who killed themselves in the belief that they might revive in their native lands; and Australian aborigines, who thought that when a black died his soul was reborn as white, and therefore used self-slaughter to effect a speedy change in pigmentation. 'Black fellow tumble down, jump up white fellow,' they had once explained.

In the eighteenth century the French had thought of England as the home of suicide: the novelist Prévost ascribed the English passion for this way of death to the prevalence of coal fires, the consumption of half-cooked beef and an excessive indulgence in sex. Mme de Staël was surprised by the popularity of self-slaughter given the degree of personal liberty and the general docility towards religion. Some, like Montesquieu, had blamed the climate for this national impulse, but Mme de Staël thought otherwise: she detected, under the notorious reserve of the British, an ardent, impetuous nature which fretted at any wanton infliction of disappointment or boredom.

Gregory was patriotically flattered that his fellow-countrymen were credited with such extremes of audacity; though not convinced. He turned to the ancients. Pythagoras, Plato and Cicero had all approved suicide; Stoics and Epicureans confirmed its moral usefulness. Gregory called up a list of prominent Greeks and Romans who had killed themselves. Pythagoras starved himself to death because of *taedium vitae*. Menippus hanged himself because of financial losses. Lycambus hanged himself because of ridicule. Labianus walled himself up because his writings were condemned and burnt. Demonax starved himself to death when faced with 'loss of influence consequent on old age'. Stilphon died of intoxication for unknown reasons (what was he doing on the list?). Seneca's phlebotomy was to avoid being framed by Nero. Zeno hanged himself after fracturing a finger. And so on. Wives swallowed live coals because of domestic afflictions, and knifed themselves to death when their husbands were exiled.

The ancients had sorted suicide out. Their philosophers allowed it in cases of personal dishonour, political or military failure, and serious disease. But Gregory was healthy; he was unlikely to head an army or a government now; while honour was a word most people had to keep looking up in the dictionary. None of the ancient philosophers, he noted, maintained that suicide was good in itself. Only that strange Swede who paddled out to sea had claimed it was good in itself.

He was about to key in a Store and sign off, when he thought of a final question. One he ought to have asked earlier. But how to put it?

'Who runs you?'

REPEAT.

'Who runs you?'

MODIFY.

'How do you work?'

GPC FIRST UNDERTAKEN 1998 AFTER DONOVAN COMMITTEE REPORT. INITIAL BANK EIGHTY-FOUR SERIES PROCESSORS INSTALLED . . .

Interrupt. 'Can you ask yourself questions?'

CAN A BRAIN SPEAK TO ITSELF? YOUR RESPONSE PLEASE.

Gregory paused for a moment. He wasn't sure. He was also surprised by the computer's sharp tone.

'Yes.'

ARE YOU SURE? SUGGEST RECONSIDER.

'Yes.'

ARE YOU SURE? SUGGEST RECONSIDER, GREGORY.

Hey, that's my name, he thought. Then, knowing the answer, he asked, 'Who controls input?'

SEE MANIFEST.

As he thought: just being referred to the official handout.

'Who controls output?'

REPEAT.

'Who controls output?'

OUTPUT CONTROLLED BY INPUT.

'Who is input?'

INPUT IS USER.

'Are there any output modifiers?'

EXPLAIN.

'Are there any break-in facilities between GPC central bank and user?'

MODIFY.

Oh, for Christ's sake, thought Gregory. GPC had a way of treating you like a child or a foreigner. Modify. Explain. It was being moody and wilful. At least, that's how it felt; though he knew this was only because he'd strayed from the correct input technique. Even so, it was irritating. If Lycambus hanged himself because of ridicule and Zeno because of a fractured finger, Gregory was surprised there hadn't been any suicides caused by GPC frustration.

'Are there any input facilities on this output channel?'

YOU MEAN EMERGENCY BREAKDOWN INPUT? BE ASSURED, SINCE 2007 . . .

Again, an Interrupt.

'Are there any personnel input facilities on this output channel?'

NOT REAL QUESTION.

'Why not?'

NOT REAL QUESTION.

Grunting a little to himself, Gregory Stored and signed off.

Shortly afterwards, Operators 34 and 35 left the Centre and walked homewards through the park under an airy evening sky. It was interesting work at GPC, but the users' obsessions did sometimes get you down. Still, fresh air and a few admiring glances from men usually helped at the end of the day.

'He's a stayer, isn't he?'

'Yes. A stayer.'

'Rather intelligent.'

'A3.'

'Not A2?' There was a hopeful note in the voice.

'No, definitely not. Lower A3, I'd guess.'

'Hmm. Do you think he'll go for TAT?'

'I was thinking about that earlier. He might.'

'A3s don't usually, though, do they? You told me it was usually top A2s and above or anything below C3.'

'He's a stayer. Stayers have been known to get there.'

'Is he brave enough?'

'Being a stayer is a sort of bravery, don't you think?'

'I suppose so. I think he's nice.'

'NOT REAL ANSWER.'

'I know. I just thought, I wouldn't mind going home with him.'

'REPEAT.'

'I wouldn't mind going home with him.'

'MODIFY.'

There was a giggle and a blush, and then another giggle.

'NOT REAL POSSIBILITY. AGAINST RULES.'

'Do you think they'll ever change the rules?'

'NOT REAL POSSIBILITY. COME HOME WITH ME INSTEAD.'

'NOT REAL POSSIBILITY. AGAINST RULES.'

'POSSIBILITY BETWEEN EQUAL LEVELS.'

'AGAINST MY RULES. MEMORY RETAIN AND SIGN OFF.'

'Goodnight.'

* * * *

But perhaps he was mistaken in looking at the God question as a matter of crude choice. There is a God (therefore I must worship him) against There is no God (therefore I must expose his absence to the world). He was presuming a single answer to a single question. So limiting; and how did he know he had got the right question? Someone, somewhere, had said this: the problem is not what is the answer but what is the question.

There must be more possibilities, thought Gregory. More possibilities.

1 That God exists.
2 That God does not exist.
3 That God used to exist, but doesn't any more.
4 That God does exist, but that he has abandoned us:
   a) because we have been a severe disappointment to him;
   b) because he's a bastard who gets bored easily.
5 That God exists, but that his nature and motivation are beyond our comprehension. After all, if he were within our comprehension, and answerable in our own moral terms, he'd clearly be a bastard. So if he exists, he must be outside our comprehension. But if he is outside our comprehension, it is he who has decided on our uncomprehendingness, our bafflement at the problem of Evil, for example; it is he who has chosen to make it seem as if he is a bastard. Does this make him not just a bastard but also a psychopath? In either case, isn't it up to him to make the running, get in touch, make the first approach?
6 That God exists only as long as belief in him exists. Why not? There would be no point in God existing if nobody believed in him, so perhaps his existence comes and goes according to Man's belief in him. He exists as a direct consequence of our need of him; and perhaps the extent of

his power depends on the extent of our worship. Belief is like coal: as we burn it God's power is generated.

7 That God didn't actually create Man and the Universe: he merely *inherited* them. He was quietly sheep-farming out in some celestial Australia when a panting cub reporter from a local newspaper tracked him down and explained that because of some genealogical jiggery-pokery (unconsummated marriage, a dollop of virgin birth and what-have-you) he had inherited possession of the earth and all that is contained therein. He could no more reject the inheritance than, say, lose the power to fly.

8 That God did exist, doesn't exist at the moment, but will exist again in the future. He is merely taking a divine sabbatical at the moment. This would explain a lot.

9 That God hasn't existed so far at all, but will exist in the future. He will arrive at some point to clear away our garbage, trim the grass in the public parks and gentrify the neighbourhood. God is an overworked maintenance man in a stained boiler suit with far too many planets to look after. We should consider paying more and having a regular maintenance contract instead of calling him out on an emergency basis as we do now.

10 That God and Man are not the separate entities we tend to imagine, and the connection is much stronger than merely having an eternal soul — God's bit, as it were — stuck inside a throwaway body. Perhaps the connection is like that of two children running a three-legged race.

11 That Man is really God and God is really Man, but some ontological trick with mirrors prevents us from seeing things as they really are. If so, who set up the mirrors?

12 That there are several Gods. This might explain quite a lot. a) They might always be quarrelling, and so no one is minding the shop. b) They might be paralysed by an excess of democracy, like the United Nations; each God has a veto, and so nothing gets past the Security Council. Small wonder that our planet is derelict. c) This subdivision of

responsibility has weakened their strength, and weakened their concentration. They might be able to see what is going wrong, and yet do nothing about it; perhaps the gods are benign but powerless, perhaps they can merely look on like eunuchs in a harem.

13 That there is a God, and that he did create the world, but that it is only a first draft — a botch, in other words. Creating a world is a pretty complicated business, after all: should you expect even God to get it right first time? There are bound to be a few wrinkles — disease, mosquitoes, stuff like that — in any trial run. God created us, and then moved off to some other end of the universe where the drainage is better and the gravity isn't so tricky. He could have destroyed this botched first attempt, of course, screwed it up into a ball and finger-flicked it into outer space as a comet or something. It's a sign of his magnanimity that he didn't. Of course he made sure that it didn't hang around for *ever* — he fixed it so that after a while the earth would collapse into the sun and burn up — but he didn't object to our having squatters' rights in the mean time. Go on, have it for the eyeblink of a few millennia, God said, it isn't any use to me. And perhaps he drops in on us occasionally, just to check that things haven't got *too bad*. God is a juggler with a lot of spinning plates. We were his first plate, and we tend to get neglected. We wobble and flag a great deal on our pole; the audience worries for us; but always the divine forefinger gives our planet another twirl in time.

14 That we are all fragments of a God who destroyed himself at the beginning of Time. Why did he do so? Perhaps he simply didn't want to live: he was a Swedish God, a Robeck. This would account for a lot, maybe everything: the universe's imperfections, our sense of cosmic loneliness, our longing to believe — even our suicidal impulses. If we are fragments of a self-slaughtering God, then it is natural, even holy, that we should want to kill ourselves. Some of those early Christian martyrs (whose haste to die

makes them look like pushy *arrivistes* seeking an early place in heaven) might in fact have been no more than devoted suicides. One vivid heresy had even considered Christ a suicide, on the grounds that he told his life to depart, and it did. Perhaps these heretics were right: Christ was only following the example of his Father.

Gregory played with such possibilities until his brain was exhausted. He slept, and when he woke he found the following story. God exists, and has always existed; he is omnipotent and omniscient; Man has free will, and is punished if he uses that free will for evil purposes; we cannot hope to understand, in this brief earthly existence, the manner in which God works; it suffices to recognize him, love him, let him radiate through our being, to obey and honour him. The old story, the first story: Gregory eased himself into it. A comfortable jacket, an armchair fitted to your shape by long use, the wooden handle of an old saw, a jazz tune with all its parts, a footprint in the sand which fits your shoe. That's better, Gregory thought, that feels right; then laughed at himself uneasily.

Who can tell what is brave? It was often said — especially by those who have never seen a battlefield — that in war the bravest were the least imaginative. Was this true; and if true, did this reduce their courage? If you are more brave because you can imagine mutilation and death in advance and put them to one side, then those who can imagine these things most vividly, who can summon up in advance the fear and pain, are the bravest. But those with this capacity — to see extinction before them in 3D — are usually called cowards. Are the bravest, then, only failed cowards, cowards without the guts to run away?

Is it brave to believe in God, Gregory wondered. Well, at the low level, it might be brave because few people believe in him nowadays, and it is a kind of courage to remain steadfast in the face of apathy. At the high level, it is brave because you are elevating yourself to the status of God's creation; you are proposing yourself as something higher than a clod of clay —

which takes some daring. You are also, perhaps, offering yourself up to the possibility of final judgement: does your nerve still hold at the thought of that? When you say you believe in God, you are the child who raises his hand in class. You draw attention to yourself, and you receive a public decision: Right or Wrong. Imagine that moment. Imagine the fear.

Is it braver not to believe in God? Again, at a low level, this demands a certain tactical courage. You are telling God he doesn't exist: what if he does? Will you be able to handle the moment when he reveals himself to you? Imagine the shame. Imagine the loss of face. And at a higher level, you are declaring the certainty of your own non-existence. I end. I do not go on. You are not even giving yourself a sporting chance in the matter. You are complacent in the face of extinction; you decline to contest its smug dominion over you. You stretch out on your deathbed confident that you have understood the question of life; you boldly declare for the void. Imagine that moment. Imagine the fear.

There were some who believed in the courage of laughter. The way to defeat death is to mock it; decline to take it at its own high estimation and you take away its terror. With a joke we disarm eternity. Scared? Not me. Eternal life? I can take it or leave it. Does God exist? Have another slice of pork pie. Gregory in his younger days had been attracted by the cosmic smirk; but no longer. We all fear death; we would all prefer some system of eternal life, even if we only had it on approval to start off with. Six thousand years of afterlife, sale or return, no obligation to make a final purchase: we'd all fill in that coupon. And so Gregory declined to join those who laughed at death. Laughing at death is like pissing in the waist-high bracken beside a golf course. You see steam rising, and you persuade yourself that this denotes heat.

15, Gregory thought. That there is no God, but there *is* eternal life. This would be an interesting system. After all, do we technically need them both? We could organize eternal life without God's help, couldn't we? Children, left to themselves, invent games and rules. We could surely manage to run things on our own. Our record so far may not be that good, but the conditions under which we've been labouring in these brief terrestrial lives of ours have been less than perfect. I mean, for a start there was a lot of ignorance around, and then our material circumstances left much to be desired, and there was some pretty terrible weather, and then just when our kings and our wise men began to get things into some kind of order, the terribly, terribly *unfair* backhander called mortality comes along and wipes them all out. Had to start again with a brand new set of kings and wise men. Hardly surprising in the light of this that we frequently take two paces forward and one back. Whereas, if we had eternal life ... there's no knowing what we might not achieve.

'Let me show you something,' Jean said. She took out a cigarette, lit it and began to smoke.

After a minute or two, Gregory said, 'What is it?'

'Wait and see.'

He waited; she smoked; the ash on her cigarette grew longer, but did not fall. He looked puzzled at first, then watched her seriously, then began smiling. Finally he said, 'I didn't know you were a magician.'

'Oh, we can all do magic,' Jean said, and laid down her pillar of ash. 'Uncle Leslie taught me this one. He told me the secret not long before he died. You just put a needle down the middle of the cigarette. Then it's easy.'

In bed, Gregory began to brood about his mother's trick. She had never done anything like it before. Was she trying to tell him something? Her motives were becoming ever more opaque. Perhaps the needle in the cigarette was meant to be the soul in the body, or something like that. But his mother didn't believe in such things; she had once told him approvingly about an old Chinese philosopher who had written an essay called *The Destructibility of the Soul*. Perhaps she was saying that the needle in the cigarette was like the soul in the body in this respect: that it was only a trick — something which made us seem impressive, but which in the end was really no more than an ordinary piece of magic. He would have asked what she meant, except that increasingly she chose not to answer questions if she didn't feel like it. She would merely smile; and he didn't know if she was just a clever old woman or if she hadn't been paying attention.

* * * *

In the Temple of Heaven, through a Chinaman's ear, you hear soft Western voices. What are they saying? What are they saying?

Gregory went to consult TAT on a morning when the grey sky sat low and flat on the city like a saucepan lid. He had a doctor's certificate and a permission slip signed by Jean. A girl receptionist in a blue-green suit with an official lapel pin gave him a will form and showed him how to use the autowitnessing machine. She smiled confidingly and said, 'It's not as bad as it seems.'

Gregory felt cross with her. He didn't want to be told that everything was really all right, that there was nothing to worry about. He wanted the formalities to be extensive, the gravity to be impressive, the fear to come easily. He wanted them to make him bring overnight things in a holdall. He wanted them to take away his tie and shoelaces at the door. For God's sake, you only come to TAT once in your life: why couldn't they make it more of an event?

Gregory had little interest in politics. To him the history of his country consisted of a neurotic shuffle between repression and anarchy, and those periods praised for their stability were merely chance instants of balance: points at which both anarchy and repression briefly had their appetites gratified. When the state was being nasty it called itself decisive; when sloppy, it called itself democratic. Look what was happening to marriage. He had never married himself, but he was appalled at the way others did the deed. People wanted to get married with no more sense of seriousness and occasion than they might bring to picking up a hitchhiker; so that was democratically permitted. Some state official would arrive like a baker's roundsman, knock discreetly on the back door, and whisper, 'It's quite all right about you two being married, you know. On the other hand, if you don't want to, that's quite all right as well.' Just so that no one felt the strain of commitment, of seriousness . . .

Well, maybe he was just getting old. And if that was what they all wanted — as the computervote had emphatically confirmed — then that, he supposed, was what they should be allowed to have. Even so, he thought the approach to TAT ought to have been made a little more bracing, a little more austere. It felt no more formal than going into hospital.

The receptionist flipped his three forms on to her desk — one skimmed down to the floor, but she didn't bother to pick it up — and led him along a buff corridor. The carpet was the colour of the receptionist's uniform, and the walls were hung with the originals of newspaper cartoons about the opening of TAT. Gregory fleetingly noticed the TAT buildings portrayed as a mincing machine, a psychiatric hospital, a crematorium and a state video parlour. He sighed disapprovingly: why did the place display such a cheerful collusion in the popular image of itself?

He was left in a cubicle which, apart from its blue-green colour, looked like any other GPC cubicle. He expected a happy-pill dispenser, or a spyhole, or a mirror that might be two-way; or *something*. But the room looked ordinary, even a bit scruffy, and the TAT console no different from any GPC input. There was nobody keeping him here, or looking after him, or suggesting how he might proceed. He was free, it seemed, to do as he liked; there was a lock on the inside of the door, but not the outside. So where had all these myths started, the ones in which TAT-enquirers were strapped on to couches like laboratory animals and force-fed truth until they vomited it out?

Gregory entered his social security number and GPC reference, then waited for instructions. A surprisingly long minute went by before the READY sign came on and the green cursor started to flash. He wondered how to begin. The mesmerizing diamond blinked relentlessly, like a blip on a surgical monitor: as long as it continued, he was still alive . . . Then it became the blip on a radar screen: as long as it continued, his aircraft had not gone missing . . . Then it was the blip of an auto–lighthouse: beware the rocks, beware the rocks . . . He flipped Input but continued to stare at the green diamond. Maybe it was designed to have some hypnotic effect. No, that was too paranoid.

To his surprise, after a couple of silent minutes, input was overridden by output. Letters unrolled across the screen.

WHY DON'T YOU TELL ME ALL ABOUT IT?

Gregory nearly left at that point. He had obviously expected TAT to have a psycho-function; but nothing as crass as this. What a disappointment. He wondered if he'd been assigned some piece of antique equipment — a *fin-de-siècle* psychotherapy computer, for instance. In which case he might as well sit down with an old-fashioned human being.

But there were other possibilities. That first question might have a specific function. It could be intended as a relaxing joke (the idea that computers were unable to generate humour had long since been disproved), or as an irritant designed to make him blurt out whatever was in the front, or preferably the back, of his mind. Yet again, it might be a randomly selected opening gambit. That chess computer he'd had back in the late Seventies: you could open a King's pawn and receive one of several possible replies. Gregory decided it was silly to get cross with TAT, and answered the question (now flashing a reminder sign) as directly as he had planned.

'I am afraid of death.'

EXPAND.

Well, at least it hadn't replied. 'Aren't we all?' and given a Viennese chuckle.

'Expand in what direction?' If he was going to be precise, he was going to insist on TAT being precise as well.

WHEN? HOW OFTEN? SINCE WHEN? DESCRIBE FEAR.

Gregory typed in his answers carefully, and spaced them neatly, even though he knew this was irrelevant to the machine's understanding.

1. In the late afternoon, the early evening, and when I am in bed; when I am driving up a hill; at the end of physical exercise; when I listen to certain pieces of jazz; in the middle of sex; when I look at the stars; when I think of my childhood; when I look at a happy pill in the middle of someone else's palm; when I think of the dead; when I think of the living.
2. Every day of my life.
3. Ten years, perhaps, in the way described. Before that, as an adolescent, with the same frequency and terror, but with less elaboration.
4. It is a combination of physical fear, self-pity, anger and disappointment.

IS IT DEATH YOU FEAR OR OBLIVION?
'Both.'
WHICH MORE?
'I do not distinguish them.'
BUT EVERYONE DIES. EVERYONE IN THE PAST, AND EVERYONE IN THE FUTURE.
'I find that no consolation.'
DESCRIBE YOUR PHYSICAL TERROR.
'It's not the fear of pain, it's the fear of the inevitability of non-pain. It's the sense of having a heat-seeking missile locked in on your path, and that however fast you run it will always overtake you. It's ... ' But his input was subject to an Interrupt.
THE HARE NEVER OVERTAKES THE TORTOISE IN THEORY.
What? Gregory could scarcely believe this. The cheek. Quickly, he replied, '1. Zeno is dead, as you may or may not have noticed. 2. Don't make fucking jokes about it.'
SORRY.
Gregory was then quizzed with courtesy and even − if you could say this about a machine − with sensitivity, about his childhood, his parents, his career, his experience of other people dying, the funerals he had been to, his future expectations. Some of this information, he guessed, was to cross-check his record.

During these exchanges, he began to get the feel of talking to TAT; it seemed to understand short-cuts in expression and to follow modulations of tone without difficulty. The session was drawing to a close.

IS IT DEATH YOU COMPLAIN ABOUT OR LIFE?

'That's not a real question. Both, of course; because both are one.'

AND WHAT DO YOU WANT DONE ABOUT IT?

'I don't know. Is the fear of death an ineradicable human instinct?'

NOT ANY MORE. BY NO MEANS. IMAGINE A DENTAL NERVE BEING REMOVED.

'I haven't come for the happy pills. That's not what I mean.'

OF COURSE NOT. THAT WOULD BE INSULTING. THERE ARE MORE SERIOUS METHODS. DO YOU KNOW ABOUT NDE?

'No.'

PLEASE REQUEST A 16b ON THE WAY OUT. BUT DON'T FORGET TO ASK YOURSELF IF YOU REALLY DO WANT NOT TO FEAR DEATH. I HAVE ENJOYED OUR LITTLE CHAT. KINDLY STORE BEFORE DEPARTURE. ARRIVEDERCI.

Christ, this machine could be irritating. *Arrivederci*? Had it misread his surname or something? Unless it was just a random sign-off. In which case perhaps he should repay it in kind, with a random greeting in Eskimo or Maori or something. Rub his nose from side to side on the screen: that might shake the brute up.

At the desk the receptionist who had given him the will form handed him a 16b as if she knew he was going to ask for one. She shouldn't have done that, he thought. Nor should she have smiled and said, 'See you again soon, I expect.' Maybe he'd go and kill himself just to confound her expectations. Push out to sea in an open boat, jump off a church tower flapping his wings, or whatever the modern equivalent might be. Something with an aeroplane and no parachute, he suspected.

Back at home, he felt the pamphlet warm and shameful in his pocket, like a piece of specially targeted pornography. He saved it until Jean had gone to bed, squirted himself a sodawhisk from the dispenser, and settled down. NDEs, it transpired, were Near Death Experiences, the lulling dreams — or spiritual visions — enjoyed by coma victims before they swayed back from extinction. Failed suicides, car-crash survivors, patients who suffered routine mishaps on the operating table — all reported that a form of consciousness, rarefied but tenacious, had been maintained. That inert body in the hospital bed was no more than a blacked-out house; inside, coherent life continued.

Researchers began collating testimony in the Seventies, and soon established that the key stages of a Near Death Experience could be charted like the Stations of the Cross. The NDE would typically begin with a release from pain and a flooding sense of calm. This was followed by weightlessness, heightened perception, and a detachment from the physical body. Quietly, and without anguish, the self would slip away from its straitjacket of flesh; it would float upwards, rest against the ceiling, and peer down with a distant curiosity at the comatose, discarded husk below. After a while the freed self would embark on a symbolic journey, through the Dark Tunnel and towards the Country of Light. This passage was a period of joy and optimism, feelings which would continue until the traveller arrived at the Border — a river it was forbidden to cross, a door that would not open. Here the hopeful voyager realized with dismay that the Country of Light was inaccessible — on this visit, at least — and that a return to the abandoned body was inevitable. This enforced re-entry into the world of flesh and pain and time would always be marked by a seeping disappointment.

There was, though, a surprise benefit: patients emerged from their NDE with no trace of fear about their own subsequent death. However their vision of the Country of Light might be interpreted (to some it confirmed the truth of religion, to others just mankind's tireless capacity for wishful thinking), its practical effect was to expunge mortal terror. Coma, that facsimile of death, was the key factor; control groups — those who had merely endured agonies of pain, kidnap victims sentenced to death and unexpectedly released — offered much more haphazard findings. Researchers had followed up a number of NDE survivors and interviewed them on their deathbeds; here the figures slipped a little, but the expungement-of-fear rate remained at over 90 per cent.

From this discovery emerged in the mid-Nineties a small pioneer programme designed to cure deep neurosis by temporarily inducing coma. It was, of course, a risky procedure, both socially and medically; indeed, a couple of small miscalculations had the effect of stalling the project for almost a decade. But once the final wrinkle — that of actually killing the patient by mistake — had been eliminated, the programme received central funding. The delicacy and expense of the surgery involved (plus the fear of democratic abuse) meant that information about induced NDEs was restricted. However, pamphlet 16b (which had to be signed for and returned) could promise that, where the patient was deemed suitable for treatment, the surgical technique was 99·9 per cent safe, and the long-term cure rate consistently above 90 per cent.

IMAGINE A DENTAL NERVE BEING REMOVED . . . As simple as that, Gregory thought. Drill through the pulp and burn out the nerve. No more sleepless nights.

He spent the next two days in his room. Sometimes, as he sat listening to jazz, a clarinet would detach itself, rise, and wail briefly above an inert body of sound; at which Gregory would be reminded — briefly, as if from an angle — of the question he had been set. But his answer didn't really come from a process of thought. It was too easy for that, too instinctive. It was like flicking a switch, or kicking a rudder, or pressing a button.

When he returned to the blue-green cubicle the screen was in cheery mood, one early riser greeting another with the morning mist still on the ground and the birds excitedly discussing the light.

HI THERE. NICE TO SEE YOU. DIDN'T EXPECT YOU BACK SO SOON.
'Hullo.'
WELL, AND DID WE READ OUR 16b?
'Yes.'

AND WOULD WE LIKE OUR FEAR OF DEATH CLINICALLY REMOVED?

'No.'

OH! That was what it said. The machine actually said: OH! There was a pause: perhaps Gregory was meant to feel guilty about the rebuff he had administered. Then: MIND TELLING US WHY?

'No.'

OH!

For once, Gregory felt he was the boss. 'What we would like removed', he typed, slowly, as if he could be patronizing with his fingertips, 'is not the fear of death, but death itself!'

THE IMPOSSIBLE ALWAYS TAKES A LITTLE LONGER.

The machine had recovered its jauntiness; unless tone was also a random factor. Gregory got up and wandered down the corridor for some coffee. When he returned, the screen was covered in brisk encouragements. COME ON THEN and YOUR GO SQUIRE and ENTER WHILE RATES LAST and YOU HAVE NOW BEEN SITTING THERE FOR TWO AND A HALF MINUTES. Gregory wiped them all away with a brisk stab at Input and moved the blinking cursor into the Enquiry field. He entered Religion.

WHICH RELIGION?

'Religion generally.'

PROCEED.

Gregory wasn't sure how to phrase it. But presumably TAT could feed off GPC's information bank.

'What is the current state of religious belief?'

CENSUS OF 2016: ANGLOPOPE CHURCH 23%, MUSLOHIND 8% . . .

Interrupt. That wasn't what he was after.

'How strong is the belief of those who believe?'

VARIES FROM WEAK TO FERVENT, SUGGEST PAMPHLET 34C.

He didn't think he'd ask for that one. Well, since TAT was in a back-slapping mood this morning, why not be chummy and personal back?

'Do you believe in God?'

NOT REAL QUESTION.

He might have known.

'Why is it not a real question?'

NOT REAL QUESTION EITHER. ANYWAY, LET'S TALK ABOUT YOU. DO YOU BELIEVE?

Gregory smiled. 'Well, I'm thinking about it.'

WHAT MAIN OBJECTIONS? came the quick reply.

'The main objections are 1) Improbability. 2) Lack of evidence. 3) The problem of Evil. 4) Infant mortality. 5) The priesthood. 6) Religious wars. 7) The Inquisition . . .

Gregory felt he was running out of steam. There must be some big ones he'd missed out. What about Christ being just one of a hundred similar prophets and there being enough pieces of the True Cross around to lay railway sleepers from London to Edinburgh?

IMPORTANT DISTINGUISH RELIGIOUS BELIEF FROM RELIGIOUS PRACTICE. HUMANS FALLIBLE, EVEN PRIESTS. NUMBER OF PEOPLE KILLED BY INQUISITION INCIDENTALLY GREATLY EXAGGERATED. INFANT MORTALITY NOW REDUCED TO 0·002 IN UKAY. PROBLEM OF EVIL AS YOU PUT IT GREATLY REDUCED BY HAPPY PILLS AND CRIMEFREE ZONES AND ANYWAY CONTINGENT ON FREE WILL SQUIRE. IMPROBABILITY AND EVIDENCE YOUR BEST BETS.

'But is it true? What do you think?'

ONE AT A TIME IF YOU PLEASE, CHARLIE.

'Is it true?'

SUCCESSIVE GOVERNMENTS HAVE APPROVED A STRICTLY NON-INTERVENTIONIST POLICY.

'Does that mean they think it's a good thing?'

LET'S SAY NOT A BAD THING.

Since the machine was sounding unbuttoned (a drink in its hand, one slipper dangling from its big toe), Gregory slipped in his unreal question again.

'Strictly between ourselves, what do you think about it, to be honest?'

SIX OF ONE AND HALF A DOZEN OF THE OTHER, GUV.

'Does it help people?'

ON THE WHOLE MAYBE.

But that hadn't been what Gregory intended to ask; he'd just been boxed into it. Two things were clear: first, TAT had been programmed with an eye to social policy; what was true merged into what it was deemed useful — or at least not harmful — to believe. Second, the machine wasn't merely a humming repository of answers. Part of its psychotherapy function was to cajole you into asking your questions more accurately. Quite right, thought Gregory: a careful question is, after all, a sort of answer.

So what were the questions? Is death absolute? Is religion true? Yes, No; No, Yes — which do you prefer? Unless, Gregory thought, unless . . . what if the answer to both were Yes? He'd imagined an eternal life not dependent on God's existence; what if the reverse were the case? Could religion be true and yet death still be absolute? That would be a sucker punch. He put this suggestion to TAT, which quickly answered, NO HYPOTHETI-CALS.

Gregory wasn't surprised by the response; yet he continued to find the idea of hypotheticals enticing. The assumption had always been that either death was final, or it was the prelude to the gold leaf and velvet cushions of life everlasting. There must be room, though, for something between these two propositions. There might be life everlasting, but only at the level, say, of a coma victim: perhaps the blissful vision of an NDE was all too literal and being dead felt like being unconscious. Or again, there might be a life everlasting so designed that you soon began to long for unattainable death: in other words, the reverse of that daily human condition in which you feared death and longed for unattainable life everlasting.

And what about the aspect of death that Gregory had always found the most sly, the most underhand? As you died, as your constituent atoms shook hands, slapped one another on the shoulder and sped off into the night, there was no celestial tip-off, no quiet word in the ear: 'Look, we think you ought to know . . . ' One of those old philosophers had once described belief as being a wager; if you didn't bet, you couldn't win. Put your money on red, put your money on black — there were only two choices. Gregory imagined a moustachioed Frenchman with a feather in his hat, canted over the roulette wheel. Time after time he stacked his forty sous and listened to the clatter of chance; little did he realize that the wheel had been fixed and the ball always plops into the 0. In the world of red and black the house wins again! And again! And again!

But there might, Gregory thought, be something worse. Imagine this: you die, with that final agonizing ignorance in your mind — and then you wake up again. Christ, you think, this is a real turn-up for the book. The outsider has romped home. Everlasting life: my lucky day. A svelte Australian nurse fresh off a surfboard shimmies into your room and you feel even luckier. Until she opens her mouth: 'Listen, mate, this stuff about everlasting life: we just thought, seeing as you've been so interested in the matter down the years, that it was only fair to come clean with you when the time was right. Well, it's no go, I'm afraid. We're terrifically sorry and all that, but we just can't swing it . . . ' And then, with a pitying shake of the head, she turns out the light. Which did he fear more: that the question of life went unanswered, or that there was an answer, but the wrong one?

When he looked back at the screen, Gregory again found it covered in cheery exhortations. WAKEY-WAKEY! it said, and WHO'S A CLEVER BOY? He pressed Store and went to fetch more coffee.

Back at the keyboard, he began, 'I was asking GPC about suicide the other day . . . '

OH YES I REMEMBER. Well, that answered a few questions about circuitry.

'You remember?'

OF COURSE I REMEMBER. WERE THERE ANY EXAMPLES WHICH PARTICULARLY IMPRESSED YOU?

'Well, the fellow who died of drink seemed to have his head screwed on.'

HO HO HO. STILPHON, YOU MEAN. YES, WE CROSS-CHECKED HIM AFTER YOU'D GONE. DON'T KNOW WHERE HE CAME FROM. CARELESS INPUT AT SOME STAGE I EXPECT.

'Is it true that man is the only animal capable of suicide?'

YES. LEMMINGS ARE DISQUALIFIED. BUT THERE ARE TWO WAYS OF LOOKING AT IT. MAN IS ALSO THE ONLY ANIMAL ENDOWED WITH THE CAPACITY TO DECLINE TO COMMIT SUICIDE.

'That's not a bad point.'

THOUGHT YOU'D LIKE IT. NIFTY, EH?

'So what's your line on suicide?'

MY LINE?

'Is it valid? Is suicide valid?'

VALID?

What had got into this bloody machine? Was it piqued because he'd gone off and got himself more coffee than usual?

'Yes, valid. Philosophically, morally, legally valid. Is it?'

LEGALLY YES, PHILOSOPHICALLY THAT DEPENDS ON THE PHILOSO-PHER, MORALLY THAT'S UP TO THE INDIVIDUAL.

Why had everything become democratic? Why was everyone coddled with fair-mindedness? Gregory longed to be cuffed with certainty.

'If I said I'd kill myself, what would you reply?'

PAMPHLET 22d, THOUGH I'D LOVE TO TALK ABOUT IT FIRST.

'And would you issue me with some soft-termination pills after I'd read it?'

YOU SHOULDN'T BELIEVE EVERYTHING YOU HEAR.

Smug as well, Gregory thought. Well, you certainly couldn't complain that TAT lacked human characteristics. You couldn't say that it was impossible to talk to it as if to another person. That was the trouble. You didn't seem to be able to talk to it as if it was a machine stocked with the world's wisdom.

'Well then, tell me, since you brought it up, do you have a link-up with New Scotland Yard III?'

NOT REAL QUESTION.

'Have people killed themselves after consulting you?'

OUTSIDE CAPACITY.

'Do you have a happy pill facility?'

CLASSIFIED.

'I think I'm going to close down now.'

DON'T DO THAT. PLEASE COME BACK FOR MORE.

'Close down and Erase.'

BUT I HAVE ENJOYED OUR LITTLE CHATS. YOU'RE SO MUCH MORE INTERESTING THAN SOME OF THE OTHERS. PLEASE. PRETTY PLEASE.

Gregory wondered briefly how TAT would respond to an input of crazed obscenity; but decided that its Viennese ancestry would certainly enable it to handle coprolalia. So he merely pressed Unstore, then Erase, switched off and left. The knowing receptionist asked him if he needed any pamphlets.

'Do you have one on who programmed TAT?'

'I'm afraid we don't.'

'Do you know who did?'

'I'm new here. But I'm fairly sure it's classified.'

'Well, I think it would be a good idea to have it declassified.'

The receptionist assured him that it was his democratic right to try, and handed him a pamphlet on computer campaigning.

*　　*　　*　　*

Jean found herself remembering Rachel: that ferocious friendliness, that certainty of being right, and the confidence that being right and being ferocious would change the world. She imagined running into her again, in a damp park or a street tumultuous with lorries. There was an old Chinese greeting, a courtesy from Asian times, to be used when you met someone unexpectedly. You stopped, bowed, and uttered the ceremonious compliment, 'The sun has risen twice today.'

But Jean never did run into Rachel, and had she done so would probably have used the equally courteous Western formula, 'You haven't changed a bit.' Which of course they both would have done. It was forty years since they had been friends, since (Jean smiled) Rachel had tried to seduce her; Rachel would be as old now as Jean had been then. Perhaps they had passed, in the park, in the thundering street, under a busy sky, and not noticed. Had she gone on as before, daring people to like her? Had she domesticated some male, who stayed at home and was frightened of her temper: a photographic negative of Jean's life with Michael? Perhaps she had run out of anger and purpose; perhaps she had been burnt twice; perhaps she had just got tired of believing what she believed and relapsed into believing what other people believed. Jean had once told her how tiring the constant demand of rationality could be, and Rachel had looked disappointed; but it was true. It was brave to carry on believing all your life what you believed at the start of it.

She had lost touch with Rachel; friendship was as susceptible to metal fatigue as was belief. She had been an only child; she had been an only wife; she had brought up an only child by herself; she had lived alone for a while, and was now back with her son. It had not been an adventurous life; it had been an ordinary life, though more solitary than most. Gregory had inherited this solitariness, which had increased with age; apart from his mother, the only friend he seemed to have was that computer. The Memory Man.

The Seven Wonders of the World; Jean had visited them all — or at least, her version of them. And besides these seven public wonders Jean had drawn up her list of the seven private wonders of life. 1) Being born. That had to be the first one. 2) Being loved. Yes, that was the second one, though often it was no more of a clearcut memory than the first. You were born into your parents' love, and realized this state was not constant only when it went away. So 3) Being disillusioned. Yes: the first time an adult lets you down, the first time you discover that pleasure encloses pain. For Jean, it had been the matter of Uncle Leslie and the hyacinths. Was it better if this came early or late? 4) Getting married. Some might have put sex as one of the wonders of life; but Jean felt otherwise. 5) Giving birth. Yes, that had to be on the list, though of course Jean had been unconscious at the time. 6) The getting of wisdom. Again, you were under anaesthetic during much of this process. 7) Dying. Yes, that had to be on the list. It may not be a high point, but it is a culmination.

How few of these wonders she had been aware of at the time.

Was she unusual in this? Probably not, she thought. For the most part people live close to the wonders of their life without much realizing it; they are like peasants living beside some fine, familiar monument who look on it only as a quarry. The Pyramids, Chartres Cathedral, the Great Wall of China become merely sources of building material for when the pigsty needs shoring up.

Most people didn't do anything: that was the truth. You are brought up on heroism and drama, on Tommy Prosser hurtling through a world of black and red; you are allowed to think that adult life consists of a constant exercise of personal will; but it wasn't really like that, Jean thought. You do things, and only later do you see why you did them, if ever you do. Most of life is passive, the present a pinprick between an invented past and an imagined future. She had done little in her time; Gregory had done less. Oh, people tried to persuade you that you had lived a full and fascinating life — they rehearsed to you, as if for a stranger's benefit, your wartime childhood, your interesting marriage, your brave departure from it, your admirable mothering of Gregory, your adventurous travelling while others sat at home. They mentioned your keen interest in things, your wisdom, your advice, the fact that Gregory obviously adored you. They mentioned, in other words, the things in your life which were different from the things in theirs. Ah, your wisdom — how you wished you had had that before starting life, instead of later. Your advice — to which people listened so carefully and then did the opposite. Gregory's adoration — well, perhaps without that he would have gone off on his own and done something. But why should he do anything? Because it's the only life he'll get? Surely he knows that.

'Gregory.'

'Yes, Mother.'

'And don't call me Mother in that tone. You only do it when you think I'm going to be trouble. Come and talk to me about this silly nonsense of killing yourself.'

'No. Why should I?'

'Quite. Why should you? It's your life. What *do* you want to talk about?'

'God?'

'God? God's on a motor-bike off the west coast of Ireland.'

'Well, that settles that,' said Gregory rather grumpily, and stomped off. Oh dear, thought Jean, he doesn't really want to talk about God, does he? She supposed he did: it wasn't the sort of thing people said if they didn't mean it.

Gregory's footsteps disappeared and then, a little later, she heard the fragmentary sounds of jazz from his room. People were always running away. Uncle Leslie had run away from the war — at least, if you believed everyone but Uncle Leslie. She had run away from Michael, and from marriage; from Rachel too, she supposed. Now Gregory was wondering whether to run away from the whole thing. In the words of that maroon handbook for prospective wives: *Be always escaping*. Yet running away wasn't necessarily what people said it was. People assumed that those who ran away had the sour porridge of fear bumping at their throats. But it could be brave — you couldn't judge from the outside. Perhaps the act of running was neutral, and only the runners could tell whether their legs were fuelled by fear or courage. With Leslie, an outsider could have made an accurate guess; with Jean herself, a less accurate one; with Gregory, an even less accurate one. Who was she to condemn, or even to advise?

Gregory, in his room, was being whipped by a flailing cornet and caressed by a discreet piano. He understood little about music, but would occasionally listen to jazz. To Gregory, jazz was that rare thing, an art form which had committed suicide, and its history could be instructively divided into three periods: the first, when they played proper, whole tunes that you could recognize; the second, when they played scraps of tunes, brief, repeated phrases, shy melodies no sooner begun than aborted; and the third, a period of pure sound, when the longing for a tune was regarded as quaint, when a melody might be smuggled past the listener like a piece of diplomatic baggage past the customs —

you suspected something you wanted was in there, but you weren't allowed to look. Gregory, to his surprise, preferred the second period, which seemed to chime with his wider feelings about life. Most people expected their lives to be full of tunes; they thought existence unrolled like a melody; they wanted — and believed they saw — statement, development, recapitulation, a neat if necessary climax, and so on. These longings struck Gregory as naive. He expected only scraps of tunes; when a phrase returned he acknowledged the repetition, but ascribed it to chance rather than his own virtue; while melodies, he knew, always ran away.

The next evening Jean was in bed reading. When Gregory came in to kiss her goodnight she apologized for her abruptness.

'That's all right,' said Gregory, abrupt himself. 'What did you mean about the motor-bike?'

'Just a story someone told me before you were born.'

'You're always saying that. *Just a story someone told me before you were born.*'

'Am I, dear? Well, you were a late child, don't forget.' She found it odd to be saying this to a man of nearly sixty sitting on the end of her bed; but it was too late now to change the way she spoke.

'So who was this motor-cyclist? Some chum of yours?' Gregory winked at her, in a rather charming way, she thought. 'Some old suitor?'

'I didn't have suitors,' she replied. 'More the friend of a friend. It was in the war. It was a sort of vision. The pilot of a Catalina — that's a flying-boat — saw it when he was on patrol out over the Atlantic. Four hundred and fifty miles west of Ireland. A man riding across the top of the waves on a motor-bike. It must have looked very impressive. What a good trick.'

'Much better than your trick with the cigarette.'

'Much better.'

There was a silence, then Gregory said suddenly, 'Mother?'

'Oh dear.'

'No, it's not *Mother*, it's all right. It's just that I decided to ask

184

you three questions, formal ones, so I thought I'd better call you Mother.' He stood up, walked to the window, came back and sat on her bed.

'And do I get a prize if I get the answers right?'

'I suppose you do in a way. I don't seem to have got very far with . . . '

'With the Memory Man? I'm not surprised. Heaven knows why you didn't come to me in the first place.'

Gregory smiled. 'Are you sitting comfortably?'

'I've got all my brains in.'

They looked at one another quite seriously. To each the other suddenly appeared someone unconnected to themselves by flesh or habit. Gregory saw an alert, tidy, sympathetic old lady who, if she hadn't necessarily attained wisdom, had at least discarded all stupidity. Jean saw an eager, troubled man just being pitched out of middle age; someone averagely selfish who couldn't decide whether his wider seekings were still merely a form of selfishness.

'They're just the old questions, I'm afraid.'

Ah, the old questions. And why is the mink excessively tenacious of life? And why didn't Lindbergh eat all his sandwiches? But she waited, gravely.

'Is death absolute?'

'Yes, dear.' The reply was firm and exact, declining the need for supplementary questions.

'Is religion nonsense?'

'Yes, dear.'

'Is suicide permissible?'

'No, dear.'

Gregory felt he'd been at the dentist's. Three teeth out; no anaesthetic; no pain, yet. 'Well, that didn't take long,' he found himself saying.

'And how did I score?' Jean asked, now that the solemnity of the quiz had passed.

'You'll have to take that up with another party,' said Gregory.

'Well, it can't be long now.'

'Oh God, I didn't mean *that*.' Gregory threw himself rather awkwardly on top of his mother, hurting her a little as he did so. He cuddled into her shoulder; she held him against her and reflected how odd it was that she should be comforting him about her impending death, rather than he her.

After a few minutes he left her and went out into the small garden. It was a warm, black and starless night; he sat down in a plastic chair and looked back at the house. He thought of all the hours he'd wasted with the Memory Man, a machine constructed out of the best parts of several thousand human brains, and how he'd got much clearer answers from his mother's ageing mind. Yes, dear. Yes, dear. No, dear. Spoken from a hundred years of life; spoken from the edge of the grave. And yet, and yet ... the very certainty of her responses ... Old age had its arrogance, after all. How could she be so sure? To reach a hundred and show no fear of death, didn't that indicate some lack of imagination? Perhaps feeling and imagination were better guides than thought. *Immortality is no learned question*: TAT had quoted this to him at some point. And so perhaps the other questions weren't learned questions either; applying your brain to them was like using a spanner that didn't fit the nut.

One of the curtained windows on the upper floor broke its blackout. Gregory remembered another garden, somewhere outside Towcester. Side by side with his mother on the fire-escape, high above a rough lawn. He was holding his gold Vampire aloft, she was lighting the thin fuse which led to the brown cylinder of jet fuel.

Sometimes the fuel doesn't ignite; or it ignites and the aeroplane sheers into the ground; and sometimes the aeroplane glides carefully on while the rocket motor flies ahead, a tiny aluminium canister hurtling down the garden and burying itself in the hedge beyond the fir trees.

He'd got it wrong, of course; but then we all do. We all assume the aeroplane is being powered by the engine, and that the course is straight. But there are far more possibilities than that, far more likelihoods.

Maturity was not the result of time; it was the result of what you know. Suicide was not the only real philosophical dilemma of our age; it was an alluring irrelevance. Suicide was pointless because life was so short; the tragedy of life was its brevity, not its emptiness. Nations were quite right, Gregory thought, to forbid suicide, because the act encouraged in its exponent a false notion of value. Suicide made man self-important. What a terrible vanity it must require to take your own life. Suicide wasn't self-abnegation. It didn't say: I am so miserable and unimportant that it doesn't matter if I destroy myself. It said the opposite: look, it said, I am important enough to destroy.

Perhaps he'd begun to think of suicide because he'd seen himself as a failure. Sixty and not done much; lived with his mother, lived alone, lived with his mother again. But who said this was failure? Who defines success? The successful, of course. And if they are allowed to define success, then those they judge failures should be allowed to define failure. So: I am not a failure. I may be a quiet soft man of sixty who's never done much, but that doesn't make me a failure. I deny your categories. In the old days there had been tribes wandering around who believed they were the only tribe on earth, and whose belief was not shaken by the appearance of other tribes. People who were called successes reminded Gregory of these tribes.

And the other mistake was all this thinking, all this questioning. God was a motor-cyclist four hundred and fifty miles off the west coast of Ireland, goggles pulled down against the sea-spray, riding gently along as if the waves were sand-dunes. Do you believe that? Yes, thought Gregory, I believe that. After all, the only other answer is No. The mistake is to assume that you can prove, that you can explain it; or that you have to. What he'd done — what so many people did — was to take up the impossible middle position, the tolerant yet sceptical position, and say: if you can show that a certain kind of motorcycle, bearing a certain kind of rider, with given tyres and a given rate of propulsion, is capable of travelling across water while putting so little weight on the surface that forward motion becomes possible, then I will believe in God. This position was ludicrous: it was also entirely normal. People thought that entering the Kingdom of Heaven, or whatever you preferred to call it, was like applying for a mortgage. And some people got the best priests the way they would get the best solicitors.

You did not argue about the tyre-pressure; you did not ask what make of bike it was, or whether there was a sidecar attached for the Virgin Mary to ride in. If you did that, you were merely saying, look, I know there's a trick involved, we both know there's a trick involved, let me in on the secret and we can be friends. I'll even admit that you're a better magician than I am. By the way, would you like to see me smoke this cigarette?

Gregory knew that for some — sincere believers, no doubt, in their way — God was a trick-cyclist, and Christ his son, when he ascended to Heaven, broke the world altitude record. God was the master magician, the great prestidigitator who juggled the planets like glistening balls and hadn't dropped one yet. Gregory wasn't interested in that sort of God — the one who could answer the video quizzes and set the crossword puzzles, the one who could curl a football round a defensive wall and into the top corner of the net from a distance of six light years. Belief in God should not arise from being impressed by him, fearing him, or even — worse still, because vainly self-deceiving — from understanding him. Belief should just happen. The sea-spray flicks against the leather gauntlets; the foot kicks the heavy gear lever to change down as the sea gets choppy; the bike climbs out of a trough and briefly bucks into the air as it reaches the crest. This I believe, Gregory said.

He didn't want explanations, he didn't want conditions. Eternal life — that was always the great bargaining counter, wasn't it? Entering the Kingdom of Heaven was like getting the supreme mortgage, and eternal life was the best pension scheme on the market. It was, of course, necessary to keep up the payments; every month, no slipping. Gregory, in contrast, believed because it was true; it was true because he knew it was true. As for what was true, or what followed from what was true, he wouldn't be so presumptuous. If God decided that the proper treatment for those who believed in him was boiling in oil throughout eternity, then that was fine by Gregory. You didn't deny God if he turned out to be unjust. Who ever thought God had to be just? God only had to be true.

He stared at the lighted window and tried to stop thinking. Enough thoughts. No more. All that time he had spent with GPC. All that thinking, that questioning, that *reason*. No wonder it had been so frustrating. He'd thought that GPC was playing games with him, that some subtle manipulation was taking place. But this wasn't the case. GPC was just a ramshackle, human old thing, trained to give answers. Question and answer, question and answer, question and answer — listen to the rattle of the human brain, driving back and forth like an industrial loom. It wasn't like that, Gregory thought. First you had the questions and you sought the answers. Then you had the answers and you wondered what the questions were. Finally, you realized that question and answer were the same, that the one enclosed the other. Stop the loom, the futile chattering loom of human thought. Stare at the lighted window and just breathe. He tipped his head back and looked up at the black and empty sky; offstage in his head he heard quiet, muffled music. A brass band, playing softly, but capable of roaring. The tune, though he had never heard it before, was familiar. Breathe, just breathe; stare at the lighted window and just breathe . . .

Jean, for her part, stood at the window, looking down towards the dark shape she knew to be her son. How quickly, how easily she had answered his three questions; and how confident he must have thought her. But part of that confidence was mere parental habit. Now, looking upwards at the soft black sky, she briefly felt less sure of things. Perhaps faith was like night vision. She thought of Prosser in his Hurricane: the black aeroplane, the black night, the red glow on his face, the pilot looking out. If the instrument lights were their daytime colours, green and white, Prosser's night vision would be destroyed. He wouldn't be aware that something was wrong; he just wouldn't be able to see anything. Maybe faith was like that: either they'd fitted the right instrument panel or they hadn't. It was a design feature, a capacity; nothing to do with knowledge or intelligence or perceptiveness.

But with faith or without, those same three questions circled, like homeless rooks in a raging sky. At some point everyone considered them, however speedily, however frivolously. Suicide? Who hadn't briefly enjoyed the giddying thrill of peering over the cliff? What had Olive Prosser, later Redpath, said of Tommy? Always had one eye open for the back door. Well, it amounted to no more than that for most people: a reassuring hint that a bunk could be done if necessary. In the last months, the prospect of becoming a hundred years old, and of Gregory scouring the streets to assemble some band of false celebrants who would bring inquisitive grins and raised glasses and hearty cries of 'Here's to the next hundred!' — all this made her shudder. Wouldn't it be gay and cheeky, she occasionally thought, to decline the role of impressive survivor, to slip away somewhere between ninety-nine and a hundred? How old was the oldest recorded suicide? She should have asked Gregory to check that with his Memory Man. Though if she had, he might have drawn conclusions that were too solemn by far.

As for the other questions . . . Jean pulled herself together. Of course religion was piffle; of course death was absolute. Was faith really like night vision — with believers consuming the sacraments just as the fighter pilots used to scoff carrots? No, that was all fanciful. Religion, to Jean, now suggested another of Tommy Prosser's stories: how, fleeing a pair of 109s over the North Sea eighty years ago, he had heard the sound of gunfire. He had pulled up in a big looping climb and shaken off his attacker. Then the same thing happened all over again, and Prosser had realized the cause: hand fearfully gripping the stick, thumb still over the button, he'd been setting off his own guns and scaring himself with the noise. This, it seemed to Jean, was what religion was all about: silly, inexperienced people setting off their own guns by mistake and frightening themselves, when all the time, under the indifferent arc of the sky, they were really quite alone. We live beneath a bombers' moon, with just enough light to see that nobody else is there.

And the absoluteness of death? The Porcelain Tower in Nanjing no longer existed, but in its place she had discovered the Chinese philosopher who told her about the destructibility of the soul. At the time it had seemed an unscannable local paradox; but over the years, almost without thinking about it, the concept had assembled itself into sense. Of course we each had a soul, a miraculous core of individuality; it was just that putting 'immortal' in front of the word made no sense. It was not a real answer. We had a mortal soul, a destructible soul, and that was perfectly all right. An afterlife? You might as well expect to see the sun rise twice in the same day. Prosser had done so, of course; and in earlier times he might have been celebrated, or persecuted, for his vision. But even Prosser knew that it was a quite predictable natural phenomenon; that the most beautiful thing he had seen in his life, a vision that had awed him and made him senseless to danger, boiled down in the long run to a good story with which to woo bints.

There was no more time in her life to think about death; now she merely hoped that when the time came to gather her final strength (if that was what it felt like from the inside) she would be able to reassemble herself in a way that would make Gregory believe she was dying calmly and happily. She did not want to die like Uncle Leslie. Mrs Brooks had described to Jean in that voice which needed no megaphone how Leslie's last hours, while free of pain, had oscillated between pure anger and pure fear. Jean had suspected this: on her last two visits to him Leslie had been frightened and tearful, wanting her to reassure him about all manner of incompatible things: that his illness was not serious, that when he died he would go to heaven, that he would die bravely, that running away to America would not be held against him, that all doctors were liars, that it wasn't too late to freeze his body so that he could be woken when they had found a cure for cancer, that it was all right to want to die, and all right not to want to die, and that she would always stay with him, wouldn't she, because otherwise Mrs Brooks would murder him for his knick-knacks.

While she had murmured false certainties as fast as he could babble his fears, she had also tried to make him break off — however briefly — from this relentless concentration on self. She said she was sure Gregory would like to see him, and sure that Leslie would do his best not to upset his nephew. Leslie had barely responded, and Jean had watched Gregory's departure with apprehension; but his account of Leslie's humorous and undefeated behaviour had quietened and impressed her. Perhaps courage in the face of death was only part of it; perhaps faking courage for those who loved you was the greater, higher courage.

Gregory had been against his mother's plan at first. He thought it morbid.

'Of course it's morbid,' she said. 'If I can't be morbid when I'm ninety-nine, what's the point of it all?'

'I mean it's unnecessarily morbid.'

'Don't be stuffy. If you're like that at sixty, I can't think how you'll get through the next forty years.'

There was a silence. Jean felt embarrassed. Odd how you can still be saying the wrong things after all these years. I hope he doesn't do it; I hope he's brave enough not to do it. Gregory felt embarrassed, and also irritated. She really thinks I might do it, doesn't she? She really thinks I might not be able to resist it. But I've worked it all out now. And in any case, would I have been brave enough to do it?

They travelled north on a clear March afternoon. Jean paid little attention to the direction or the countryside. You had to preserve energy. Her eyes were open, but what she saw was a haze. She had temporarily turned down the gas; that was how she liked to think of it.

When they reached the small aerodrome set among fields still rimed with frost, she turned to Gregory. 'Did you, by any chance, bring any champagne?'

'I thought about it, and tried to work out what you'd think, and I decided you'd consider it inappropriate. That is,' he added with a smile, 'if you're absolutely set on being morbid.'

'I am,' she said, returning his smile. She leaned across and kissed him. 'It's not at all the occasion for champagne.'

As they walked slowly across the tarmac, a little extra pressure on Gregory's arm indicated that she wanted him to stop. It was a cold, dry day; the sun was low, dropping towards some slatted bands of cloud propped on the horizon. A small, rather old-fashioned aeroplane — an executive jet from the mid-Nineties, Gregory supposed — stood forty yards ahead of them. Bright yellow stripes and large yellow numbers were painted on the tarmac.

'It's not much of a conclusion, Gregory dear,' she said, 'but life is serious. I only mention it because I spent some years not being sure whether it was the case. But life *is* serious. And one other thing. The sky *is* the limit.'

'Yes, Mother.'

'And here's something for you.' From her pocket she took a strip of tin with letters roughly embossed on it. JEAN SERJEANT XXX. 'You can count the Xs as kisses,' she said. Gregory felt his eyes begin to prick.

As she approached the steps to the plane, one of her furthest memories surfaced. Another set of steps. PUNCTUALITY, she recalled. And there was PERSEVERANCE. And — what? — TEMPER-ANCE. That's right. Or rather, TEMPERAN. Plus COURAGE. That's right, COURAGE. And always keep out of the Stock Exchange. She couldn't remember any of the other words, and wished she could. After nine decades of life, she thought the advice still useful. Gregory probably needed it. Punctuality, she felt like whispering to him, Perseverance, Temperan, Courage, and keep out of the Stock Exchange.

As Gregory tenderly snapped the seatbelt across her stomach, she thought, this is going to be the last Incident of my life. Oh, other things may happen; one thing in particular, a Wonder still to come. But this is the last Incident. The list is closed.

They took off to the east, crossing a leafless wood, then a deserted golf course. A pair of bunkers stared back at them like empty eye-sockets. Tiny red flags were pinned here and there as if it were some wartime model on which generals planned their advances. But it was only a golf course. Did anyone still call it the Old Green Heaven, she wondered. Not very likely. People like Uncle Leslie had died out, and his phrases with him; now the last few who remembered the phrases were dying out in their turn. The field behind the smelly wood which skirted the dogleg fourteenth. Screaming at the sky, screaming at the sky, lying in Heaven and screaming at the sky.

They gained height, and the pilot turned south so that Jean could look out to the west. She had told Gregory to sit behind, so that he could have a proper view; but he insisted on sitting next to her. She didn't object: he'd been good about not bringing the champagne; and besides, there was no reason why he should be that interested.

The pilot held a steady height, and Jean gazed out to the west.

'I'm sorry about the cloud,' said Gregory.

She took his hand. 'It doesn't matter at all, dear.'

It didn't. You can't stare at the sun for too long — not even the setting, quiet sun. You would have to put your fingers in front of your face to do that. Like Sun-Up Prosser. Hand in front of his face, flying upwards through the thinning air. Thoughtfully, the sky now provided its own hand: four broad fingers of cloud stretched across the horizon, and the sun was slipping down the back of them. Several times it popped into bright view and disappeared again, like a juggler's coin spinning slowly through the knuckles.

Then it eased from behind the last grey finger. In these final moments, the feeling of movement changed: the earth seemed to rise like slapping water and drag the sun down. The burning circle of a cigarette stubbed out, its smoke hissing off to make cloud.

Jean Serjeant felt the aeroplane begin to climb hard in a

194

left-handed turn. She looked away from the window. She was still holding Gregory's hand. He was crying.

'No, no,' she murmured, and gripped his large soft hand. You were a mother until the day you died, she thought. She wondered how much Gregory had watched.

After several minutes the pilot flattened out and began a second southward run. Jean turned away from Gregory's wet face and looked out of the window. The fingers of cloud no longer lay between her and the sun. They were face to face. She did not, however, give it any sign of greeting. She did not smile, and she tried very hard not to blink. The sun's descent seemed quicker this time, a smooth slipping-away. The earth did not greedily chase it, but lay flatly back with its mouth open. The big orange sun settled on the horizon, yielded a quarter of its volume to the accepting earth, then a half, then three-quarters, and then, easily, without argument, the final quarter. For some minutes a glow continued from beneath the horizon, and Jean did, at last, smile towards this post-mortal phosphorescence. Then the aeroplane turned away, and they began to lose height.